Wicked Tales Four:

Worlds of Imagination

by **Ed Wicke**

Wicked

6 The Three Little ~~Pigs~~ Kittens

Awwww. Three cute kittens armed with water pistols, catapults, Kalashnikov rifles, rocket launchers.... Maybe the big, bad wolf won't blow their house down after all.

20 SuperBaby

SuperBaby's parents don't know that he can read, or that his best friends are a rat, a mouse, a cat, a brick and an empty cereal box. They don't even know he can fly.

39 The Ten Wishes

Be very careful what you wish for. And make sure the fairy isn't listening to Troll Rock at the time.

68 Trog the Thunderdog

Trog used to be Rover. The Witch has given up **not** eating children. The Littlest Thundertroll is in trouble for throwing prawn sweets at the Queen. There's a lightning bolt stuck in a tornado. Dogs shouldn't try to ride bicycles. Are you confused yet?

Tales Four

97 Georgina and
the Dragon

There's a very special amusement park where unwanted princes and princesses can be disposed of. But some princesses are harder to get rid of than others. And some dragons aren't as fearsome as they should be.

121 The Snow Queen

She's the biggest pop star in the universe and everybody loves her madly, including a Troll who wants to marry her and take her back to his cave to do the cleaning and look after Granny. He's unlikely to succeed, though: the Snow Queen has a zillion dollars, a magic wand and a dark, dark secret.

145 Sleeping Beauty featuring the
~~Four~~ Seven Easter Bunnies

A tale of crunchy carrots, chainsaws and camaraderie, with characters who are cute, cruel, credulous, conniving, cunning, contrary or crazed. You might need a dictionary.

Note to the reader:

These stories are brilliant for reading out loud. Tell them to your teacher, your Grandpa or a chicken. Even better, get your teacher to read them to a chicken while the chicken is reading them to your Grandpa.

But whether you read them in your head or tell them out loud to the slugs in your garden, _you need to do the voices_. Just go for it! Make the Kittens sound cute, the Wolf hungry, the Bunnies cool and the Troll short and broad and slow at thinking. Let that Dragon roar and make the Snow Queen sound like the vain Pop Diva she is.

I've included a guide to the voices for each story. However, these are only _my_ ideas, and there's no reason why the Easter Bunny in your head should sound exactly like the one in mine...

Some other books by Ed Wicke:
Wicked Tales
Wicked Tales Two: Even Wickeder Tales
Wicked Tales Three: The Witch's Library
The Game of Pirate
Billy Jones, King of the Goblins
Akayzia Adams and the Masterdragon's Secret
Akayzia Adams and the Mirrors Of Darkness
Mattie and the Highwaymen
Bullies
Nicklus
The Muselings
Screeps

Ed Wicke

Wicked Tales Four:
Worlds of Imagination

Dedicated to the wonderful staff and volunteers I work with at St Michael's Hospice, Basingstoke, and especially those who have had to put up with me the most - Elene, Lisa, Julie, Nikki, Danny, Mo, Michelle, Becky, Helen, Grace, Gill, Heather, other Mo (night owl!), Sue, Jenny, Cathy, Roberta, Lorraine, Hazel, Gail, Sandy, Mary, Angela, Jane, Paul, Thelma, Ingrid, Janet, Marie, a couple of Kates and two Shelias.

And to my friends who give me good advice that I really ought to follow! – this time, especially Nadia & Deijane & Christine.

Published by BlacknBlue Press UK
13 Dellands, Overton, Hampshire, England
blacknbluepress@hotmail.com

This book copyright © May 2012	Ed Wicke (edddwicke@hotmail.com)
Cover copyright © May 2012	Janine Douglas
Illustrations copyright © May 2012	Janine Douglas
	Simona Shakeshaft
	Marta Maestro Remuzgo
	Rachel Wicke Eggington
	David Eggington (5 years)
	Alice Wicke McKinstrie
	Ben McKinstrie
	Ara McKinstrie (3 years)
	Maverick McKinstrie (13 months)
	Ed Wicke (ancient)

ISBN 978-0-9840718-7-6

The Three Little ~~Pigs~~ Kittens

The voices

The Kittens are very, very cute and they know it. They have a way of fastening their big kitty eyes on your own which makes you want to give them anything they ask for. Even when they threaten you with tactical nuclear weapons, you find yourself exclaiming, "Awwwww! Aren't they sweet!" (Note: the youngest child in a family is often a kitten and can be very useful for acquiring tatty bits of bric-a-brac or sweets past their sell-by date).

The Mother Cat and Pig sound like all mothers everywhere when they're getting ready to go out to a party and you're bothering them with silly things like "I haven't been fed today" or "The babysitter looks awfully like a wolf with a flamethrower".

The Wolf has a big, furry, deep, proud, growly voice. He sounds tough and mean: the sort of wolf who carries a handgun in the pocket of his sheepskin coat and has a scary, devious knife-throwing girlfriend from Eastern Europe. He intends to have his bacon sandwich and isn't going to take **Meow** for an answer.

The Kind Old Ladies are the ones you see in charity shops and at every village fete. They move very slowly and smell of lavender. They are sweet and friendly and helpful, and sound like they're a hundred years old. They're remarkably creative at addition, subtraction and dropping your money on the ground. You're always surprised when they reach into the box under the table and bring out a Samurai sword or a shoulder-held missile launcher.

The Truck Drivers are good old boys who'd be glad to help anybody, so long as there's a handful of money passed over. They like Country & Western music. They laugh at anything small and squashable, such as kittens. This time they don't laugh for long.

The story

In fond memory of "Little Trace" Whetnall, January 2008.

~~Once upon a time there were three little pigs who were sent out into the world.~~

~~'Are we off to seek our fortunes, mother?' they asked.~~

~~'No, I'm sending you away to save your pink piggy skins. Your father was made into sausages last week and the same will happen to you if you don't leg it.'~~

~~She pushed them out the gate of the pigpen, waved goodbye, then put on makeup and high heels and went out to a dance club, where she partied all night long.~~

*No, that won't work. There's no point in telling you a story about three cute little piggies trying to escape a big bad wolf. You probably eat more pigs than any wolf does! Bacon, sausages, pork pies, sausage rolls…. So they **weren't** pigs. They were kittens. Very cute kittens.*

I'll start again… Once upon a time there were three little ~~pigs~~ kittens who were sent out into the world.

'Are we off to seek our fortunes, mother?' they mewed as she packed their belongings into three sweet, tiny mouse-skin bags.

'That's right, dears.'

'Will you give us a gold coin each, like in the stories?'

'Don't be silly. Pigs don't have money - I mean, *kittens* don't have money!'

She pushed them out of the house, waved goodbye, then put on makeup and high heels before going out to a dance club called The Wall, where she partied all night long with the other cool cats.

A straw house

As the kittens were walking along the road, they met a man with a truckload of straw.

'Please, sir: can we have some of your straw to build a house with?' they mewed.

The man laughed at them. 'Don't be silly,' he said. 'This straw costs two copper coins for every bale. Pigs don't have money!'

'We're not pigs. We're kittens. And very cute ones, too.'

They looked up at him sweetly. Very sweetly. So sweetly it would probably make you cry. But he was a big, tough guy who never cried, except when he was listening to Country and Western music.

'Kittens don't have money either,' he sneered.

They looked at him even more sweetly and said in cute little voices, 'But if you don't give us any straw, we can't build a house. So we'll get cold and wet and sad, and the big bad wolf will come and eat us and we'll die and then we'll come back and haunt you every night as kitten ghosts.'

'- Yeah, and because we're ghosts we'll able to wander around inside your body.'

'- We'll meow rude things inside your head!'

'- We'll eat your thoughts so when you try to think of things, all you remember is *Me-ow.*'

'- We'll use your brain as a kitty litter tray!'

'- We'll do ghost kitty wee-wees in your ears!'

'- Pleeeease give us some straw....'

The man threw a few bales of straw off the truck and drove away very fast.

'Mew!' cried the three kittens sadly. 'Please could someone come... and lift this big bale of straw off us... we're getting squashed very flat...'

Big bad wolf

Later that evening, a big and notoriously bad wolf came prowling by.

'Ah ha!' he exclaimed. 'Someone's building a house out of straw, hey? Little pigs, little pigs, let me come in!'

'Mew!' said one of the bales of straw.

'No,' said the wolf firmly. 'It's "*Not by the hair of my chinny-chin-chin*". Not *mew.*'

'Help!' said the bale of straw.

'Never mind,' said the wolf. 'Let's not waste time. I'll huff and I'll puff and I'll blow your house down!'

He began huffing and puffing, but it was no good of course. There's no way a wolf can blow down a house, even a house made of straw – which simply goes to show that you shouldn't believe half the stories you read in newspapers.

'Hmmm,' he said. 'I'll have to get some tools. You wait here, little pigs.'

'Mew! Help!' said the bale of straw.

He returned with a bread knife, a Samurai sword, a

crowbar and a chocolate Easter egg he'd been given by four bunnies. He began humming a happy song about ham sandwiches as he placed a loaf of bread on a bale of straw and cut off two slices of bread.

'Mustard!' he exclaimed. 'I forgot the mustard!'

He was so annoyed with himself that he threw down the knife... which cut through the string that held the bale of straw together... causing the bale to fall apart... and freeing three rather squashed-looking kittens.

'Thank you!' they mewed sweetly to the wolf.

'What?' he roared. 'You aren't pigs?'

'No, we're cute kittens. *Very* cute kittens. Could you help us build a house out of straw, please? Pretty please?'

But the wolf snarled and leapt upon them and...

... And he would have eaten them up if this had been a story about three little pigs. But the kittens dodged between his legs and ran away into the forest, where they climbed a tall tree and spent the night caterwauling sadly at the moon.

The wolf went home and made a sausage sandwich for his supper.

A house of sticks

The next day, the three little kittens made the rounds of charity shops. They would find something they wanted and then look at it very sadly for a long time until a kind old lady said, 'Do you like that, my dears?'

They would look up at her with their big eyes and nod hopefully.

'Don't you have any money, dears?'

They would shake their heads sadly and their big eyes would fill with cute little tears.

'Awwww, you can have it for nothing, then.'

'Mew! Thank you!' they would say and snatch the little trinket from the shelf and drop it into a big bag full of clinking trinkets.

'Is there anything else you'd like, dears?'

'Mew... Have you got any guns?'

That afternoon they were walking along the road again, dragging their huge bags full of old tat, when a man drove past with a truckload of sticks.

'Please, sir: can we have some of your sticks to build a house with?' they mewed.

The man laughed at them. 'Don't be silly,' he said. 'These sticks costs three copper coins for every bundle. Pigs don't have money!'

'We're not pigs. We're very cute kittens.'

'Kittens don't have money either,' he said in a *tough-guy-who-drives-a-truck-and-squashes-little-animals* voice.

They said sweetly, 'But if you don't give us any sticks, we can't build a house. So we'll get cold and wet and sad, and the big bad wolf will come and eat us and we'll die and then we'll come back as zombie kittens and eat you alive.'

'- Yeah, we'll eat you a mouthful at a time, night after night. Starting with any little dangly bits.'

'- And you won't be able to invite your friends around to dinner because we'll be doing our stiff-legged zombie kitten walk all through the house.'

'- And you won't be able to kill us, because we'll already be dead!'

'- Pleeeeease can we have some sticks?'

The man threw a few bundles of sticks off the truck and drove off as fast as he could.

'Mew!' cried the three kittens sadly. 'Please could someone come... and lift these heavy sticks off us... we're getting squashed very flat again...'

Big bad wolf against superior firepower

Later that evening, the wolf came prowling around again. He stopped by a cute little house that had been made out of interlocking sticks. He called out:

'Ah ha! Little pigs, little pigs, let me come in!'

'We're not pigs!' said three voices from inside the house.

'You can't fool me,' said the wolf. 'I'll huff and I'll puff and I'll blow your house down!'

He began huffing and puffing, but it was no good of course. There's no way a wolf can blow down a house made from sticks – which simply goes to show that you shouldn't believe half the things told you by politicians.

'Hmmm,' he said. 'I'll have to get some tools. You wait here, little pigs.'

'Not pigs! **Kittens!**'

He returned with two slices of bread, a flamethrower and a chainsaw he had borrowed from four bunnies. He began humming a happy song about bacon sandwiches as he lit the flamethrower.

'I remembered the mustard this time!' he called as he turned the fire towards the house made of sticks.

… And the result would have been a lovely roast pork dinner if this had been a story about three little pigs. But the kittens poked out a big gun barrel between the sticks and pressed a trigger, squirting the wolf and his flamethrower with a lot of rather nasty-smelling liquid.

'Yuk! What's that?' he shouted.

'Mew. It's a super soaker full of caterpillar catsup.'

The wolf threw his flamethrower to one side and picked up the chainsaw. 'Okay, pigs,' he said, 'see if you can put *this* out!'

He started the chainsaw and stepped toward the house of sticks. Then three catapults were poked out from between the sticks, and the kittens began shooting caterpillars, catkins, catfish, Catherine wheels, catalogues, catnip, cattails and cathedrals (well, models of cathedrals inside glass paperweights).

'Ouch!' said the wolf several times. But he didn't stop chainsawing his way through the sticks. 'I'm coming, little pigs!' he shouted. 'I'm – cff chk cff cff hckff hckff – what are you shooting now?'

'Catarrh,' said a cute little voice.

Another added, 'Mew – and you'd better run before we shoot you with catastrophes!'

But the chainsaw had buzzed all the way through the sticks now, and it would have been curtains and catcalls for the kittens. But as the wolf sprang upon them, he noticed all the sweet trinkets lined up on the stick mantelpiece: deformed glass angels, pottery owls with cross eyes, bad models of historic buildings, one-legged ugly ducklings, untrustworthy-looking Russian dolls....

'Hey!' said the wolf. 'Check out the great ornaments!'

Meanwhile, the kittens had escaped into the forest, where they climbed a different tall tree and spent the night caterwauling at the moon again.

The wolf took the trinkets home and had a pork pie for his supper.

A house of bricks this time

The next day, the three little kittens went to several coffee mornings and wandered about the loaded tables. They found lots of manky bric-a-brac to buy.

Look at it very sadly with our big, cute kitty eyes.

Kind old lady says, 'Do you like that, dears?'
Look up at her with big eyes. Nod our heads hopefully.
'Don't you have any money, dears?'
Shake our heads sadly.
'Awwwww. You can have it for nothing, then.'
'Mew! Thank you!'
Snatch, grab, into the bag.
'Is there anything else you'd like, dears?'
'Mew... Have you got any Kalashnikov rifles?'

That afternoon they were walking along the road again, dragging even bigger bags, when a man drove past with a truckload of bricks.

'Please, sir: can we have some of your bricks to build a house with?' they mewed.

The man laughed at them. 'Don't be silly,' he said. 'These bricks costs a silver coin per hundred. Pigs don't have money!'

'We're not pigs. We're kittens. And very cute ones, too. Everyone loves us and gives us what we ask for....'

'Kittens don't have money either,' he said. 'Not even cute ones. And you kittens had better stay away from this road, because I like turning kittens into flat, furry mittens. These wheels were made for squashing. Ha!'

They mewed sadly, 'But if you don't give us any bricks, we can't build a house. So we'll get cold and wet and sad, and the big bad wolf will come and eat us and we'll die and then we'll come back as vampire kittens and suck your blood.'

'- Yeah, we'll fly down the chimney as soon as you turn on your favourite TV program.'

'- And you'll find it hard to sleep because you'll know we're hanging upside down somewhere, planning to fly in for a little snack.'

'- We'll suck out a little blood every day, until you're all shrivelled up like a prune.'

'– You'll never get a girlfriend because she'll be worried we'll drink her blood as well.'

'– Pleeeeease can we have some bricks?'

The man threw a pallet of bricks off the truck and drove away with a screeching of tyres.

'Mew!' cried the three kittens sadly. 'Please could someone come... and lift these very heavy bricks off us... we're getting squashed very flat... again...'

Big bad wolf encore with bigger weapons

Later that evening, the wolf came prowling by again. He stopped by a cute little brick house with a mouse-shaped mailbox and beautiful stained glass windows.

'Ah ha!' he exclaimed. 'Little pigs, little pigs, let me come in!'

'Come in!' called three cute kitten voices from inside.

'You can't trick me like that,' said the wolf. 'I'll huff and I'll puff and I'll blow your house down!'

He began huffing and puffing, but it was no good of course. There's no way a wolf can blow down a house made from bricks – which shows that you shouldn't be-lieve anything a storyteller tells you. Unless it's me.

'Hmmm,' he said. 'I'll have to get some tools. You wait here, little pigs.'

He returned with a bowl of noodles, some sweet chili sauce and a sledgehammer. He hummed a happy song about sweet and sour pork as he began smashing a hole in the house.

'Take that!' mewed a tiny voice, and a catapult shot something small, with horns and four legs, high into the air. It dropped from the sky onto the wolf's head.

'Moo,' it said in a tiny, surprised voice.

Several cow-shaped ornaments followed.

The wolf howled, 'Yowwww! You're catapulting cattle!' He threw his sledgehammer to one side and pulled a big automatic pistol from his sheepskin jacket. 'Okay, pigs! No more Mr Nice Guy!'

He began firing at the cute stained-glass windows, which tinkled merrily as they smashed.

'Mew! Ouch!' called three voices. Then three machine guns appeared at the broken windows and began spraying the countryside with bullets.

The wolf threw himself into a ditch just in time. 'Think you're tough, do you, pigs?' he shouted. 'Well, have a taste of this!'

A grenade landed on the tiled roof of the house, bounced about a bit and blew a hole in the roof.

'Mew! Ouch!' called three voices again. Then one voice added sadly, 'Help! We've run out of bullets!'

But as the wolf leapt from the ditch and ran towards the house, the guns began spewing out scarier things than bullets, such as:

Support stockings
Second hand false teeth
Dollies with heads that won't stay on
Bent reading glasses
Jigsaw puzzles with two pieces missing
Cassette tapes of singers your gran used to like
Rubber ducks that always float on their side in the bath
Paintings of places you never want to visit
Old books with pages falling out
Russian dolls with scary faces
Teddy bears with their stuffing leaking out

'Noooo!' howled the wolf. He ran away... but returned half an hour later, driving an armoured tank. And that would have been the end of the story, if it had been about three little pigs. But as he blasted the brick house to smithereens, the three little kittens ran under the tank and away into the forest where – you guessed it - they climbed yet another tall tree and spent the night caterwauling at the moon again.

This is a tank by David

'I'll be back!' promised the wolf. He went home and had takeaway pork balls with fried rice and crispy noodles for his supper.

Preparing for the next battle...

The next day was Saturday, and it was raining: so of course there was a big village fete that weekend. The kittens went to the fete and found a wet trinkets stall being looked after by a sweet-faced lady wearing a purple hat. They gathered by the table, dripping with rain. They gazed longingly at the dripping trinkets, then looked sadly up at the kind old woman.

'Would you like to buy some bric-a-brac, dears?'

They nodded their heads and looked at her with their big, hopeful eyes.

'Do you have any money?'

They shook their heads and looked at her sadly.

'Would you like to have them for free?'

They shook their heads once more. 'Mew. We don't have anywhere to put them. Mew.' They looked down at the ground with their big eyes this time, as if they were sad and lonely and shy and embarrassed.

'Where do you live, little dears?'

They whispered, 'We live in a cold, slimy ditch.'

'- We have to eat slugs for dinner.'

'- The frogs say mean things to us.'

'- And the big bad wolf is trying to get us.'

The lady sighed and said, 'Awwww, you poor cute kittens! Would you like to come live with *me*?'

They nodded sweetly and asked in very cute voices:

'Mew! Do you have a nice house, with curtains we can climb?'

'- Chairs we can scratch?'

'- Carpets we can make kitty messes on?'

'- Do you have a bird table?'

'- And no dog?'

'- Trinkets on the mantelpiece we can knock off in a cute way?'

The kind old lady laughed and said, 'Of course! Is there anything else you need?'

The kittens thought hard. Then they asked sweetly:

'Have you got any anti-tank missiles?'

SuperBaby

The voices

SuperBaby sounds like a baby. He's cute and friendly and doesn't understand most of what he reads in the newspaper. He knows his parents wouldn't be able to cope with his super powers, so he just babbles to them in baby talk. Like all babies, he gets excited very quickly and sad very quickly. He'll fall asleep half way through a conversation, or wake up at three in the morning wanting to read his cereal box.

Superbaby's parents talk to him in that over-bright, over-simple way that adoring adults use with babies. When talking to one another, **The father** sounds puzzled and a little annoyed about always getting the blame for things SuperBaby does. **The mother** sounds fussy. **Grandma** sounds like she thinks she knows best.

Cat the Cat is a relaxed, friendly cat who spends a lot of time sleeping. She has a high, sweet, mewing voice and makes cute *Prrrrrp!* sounds at SuperBaby's window when she wants to come in. She's calm and sensible and loyal. She doesn't understand why the baby won't eat the mouse she brings him, but now that Mick is the baby's friend, she'll protect the mouse with her life.

Mick the Mouse's squeaks always sound rather scared, because being a mouse *is* scary - what with owls and cats and foxes and mousetraps and burglars who might steal your whiskers.

Rocky the Rat – well, he's a bit rough and ready, right? If you want some second hand greasy chips, pickled onions or water pistols, Rocky's your man. Or rat.

Ben the Box says nothing at all. Because he's a box.

The story

At half past midnight, SuperBaby was born.

He was quite surprised to be out in the cold air and wondered where all the nice warm water and gurgling sounds had gone. He didn't like the light much, either.

He kept his eyes shut and held his breath. The nurse gave him a little push and a poke, to get him to breathe. He didn't like *that* either and held his breath even more. So the nurse picked him up and gave him a tiny slap on his tiny botty.

He *really* didn't like *that*, so he started crying (and breathing). And as soon as the nurse turned her back, he reached out and gave *her* a slap on the botty, too!

'Ouch!' she said, turning around and staring at SuperBaby's father. She added, 'You slapped me on the -'; and then she pointed at the place of the slap.

'It wasn't me!' said SuperBaby's father.

The nurse wagged her finger at him and said, 'Well, it certainly wasn't the baby, was it?'

'But – but – I didn't do it!' said the father. But no one believed him, and he got the blame for something SuperBaby had done. Not for the last time!

Cat the Cat and Mick the Mouse

You always remember your first friend, even if she's rather naughty. SuperBaby's first friend was a cat who was very good at putting holes in curtains, stockings and mice. SuperBaby didn't understand about names yet, so he called his friend Cat the Cat.

One morning Cat the Cat appeared on the window ledge outside SuperBaby's window and called to him: '*Prrrrpppp!*' SuperBaby flew to the window, opened it and flew back to bed. The cat came in, carrying something in her mouth.

'Got a present for you,' said Cat the Cat. 'Thought you might be getting tired of milk.'

She dropped a dazed-looking mouse into SuperBaby's cot. 'Get your teeth into that!' she said.

'I haven't got any teeth yet,' said SuperBaby. 'What's that furry thing?'

'A mouse,' said Cat the Cat. 'Very tasty they are, too. If you don't want it, I'll eat it.'

The mouse looked up at SuperBaby and gave a sad little squeak.

SuperBaby said to the mouse, 'It's all right. No one's going to eat you. You can be my second friend. I'll call you Mick the Mouse!'

Mick the Mouse was rather tired after his exciting morning. He had been chased – caught – let go – caught again – carried up a tree – across to the window ledge – then dropped into a baby's cot. So he curled up next to SuperBaby and fell into a lovely, deep sleep.

Cat the Cat shook her head. 'Waste of a good snack!' she grumbled. Then she curled up on the other side of the baby and dozed off, too.

SuperBaby smiled as he also fell asleep. He had two friends now – life was good!

Half an hour later they were awakened by a scream: *'Help! A mouse! There's a mouse in the baby's bed!'*

SuperBaby woke to find his mother pointing at him. Her face was white and she was shouting very loudly, so he started to cry. His father ran in, picked up Mick the Mouse and threw him out the window.

His mother said to his father, 'Look what happens when I leave you alone with the baby! I come back an hour later and you've left a window open – *and* you've let the cat get onto the baby's bed, *and* a mouse as well!'

'But I didn't open the window,' said the father.

'Well, the baby didn't do it!'

The father sighed. He was in trouble again for something SuperBaby had done. Not for the last time!

After a while, Cat the Cat meowed at the window again: so the baby flew across to let her in.

'Did you find Mick the Mouse?' asked SuperBaby.

'Yep,' said the cat. 'And he was delicious!' She patted her tummy and winked at the baby.

SuperBaby began to cry. 'You ate my friend!' he said.

'Nah – I was just pretending,' said the cat. 'I couldn't find him.'

SuperBaby cried even louder. 'We've lost Mick the Mouse!' he howled. And because he was a baby, he cried for a long time until his mother came and picked him up – and chased the cat out the door again.

SuperBaby had a good morning after that, being played with and fed and changed and played with and fed and… you get the idea. In the late afternoon, the children were going home from school and his mother carried him to the window so he could watch them passing. He kicked his little legs to show her that he wanted to go running and playing like the big children.

'How sweet!' she said. 'But you'll have to wait another year before you can do that!'

Wisely, he said nothing. He didn't want to frighten his parents.

Just then a stone came flying through the air and bounced off the window pane, startling SuperBaby so that he began to cry.

'That's the bad boy from next door!' she said. 'He's always throwing stones at the squirrels. It's very naughty of him, and he might hurt someone. Nap time, baby.'

SuperBaby had a good nap. When he woke up, he needed his nappy changing. He was just about to make that special baby cry that means 'Help! Messy nappy!' when he heard a sad sound from outside.

It was Cat the Cat mewing and howling! SuperBaby must save her! So he flew to the window, opened it and flew out.

Poor Cat the Cat was trapped in a corner of next door's garden, against the fence. She had found Mick the Mouse, who was trying to hide behind her as the boy next door pelted them with stones and dirt. They were both dodging from side to side, looking scared.

This was a job for SuperBaby! He flew over the boy's head and shouted, 'Stop that!'

The boy looked all around. No one was there. He picked up another stone.

SuperBaby shouted, 'Put that stone down!'

The boy looked around again. He was worried. He whispered, 'Is that a ghost talking?' But he threw the stone anyway.

SuperBaby said sternly, 'Don't throw stones. It's a bad thing to do!'

'Ha!' said the boy. 'You can't stop me, ghost!' He picked up even more stones.

'You'll be sorry!' warned SuperBaby.

'No I won't!' said the boy.

SuperBaby gave a little wiggle and his messy nappy slipped off his legs and landed upside down on the boy's head.

The boy screamed and ran inside, with the nappy still on his head.

'I said you'd be sorry!' SuperBaby shouted after him.

SuperBaby made a house for Mick the Mouse in the back of a cupboard which was full of the zillion fluffy toys that people had given him. He didn't like fluffy toys and always threw them out of his cot.

He was especially suspicious of a cute green teddy bear that Grandma had given him. He called it Evil Teddy, and every time Grandma came she found Evil Teddy in a different place: in the bin in SuperBaby's room… hanging from a branch of the tree outside… on the roof… upside down in the toilet…

His father was always blamed for this. Not for the last time!

Ben the Box and Rocky the Rat

You always remember your first baby cereal. SuperBaby's mother had bought a small box of it, and showed it to the baby. He wasn't sure what he was supposed to do, so he made the *ooh* and *googoo* and *bah* sounds he had been practising that morning so that he could pretend he couldn't talk.

'Clever baby!' she said. 'He knows it's something nice!'

And it *was* nice – it was the most wonderful thing he'd ever tasted! He cried when it was all gone and held out his little hands for the box until she gave it to him.

'Look, baby!' she said, pointing at the words on the box. 'It has *sugar* in it, and *rice* and *milk powder*! You like all those!'

SuperBaby stared at the squiggles on the box. So *that's* what all the funny marks on boxes and newspapers and books were about! They meant something! They were *words*! Hooray! Now when he was bored in his cot, he could teach himself to read! He began running one tiny finger across the letters.

'Ah, how sweet - he's pretending to read!' said his mother.

And from that day on, he took Ben the Box with him everywhere, reading him again and again. He especially loved the word "sugar". At night he slept with Ben the Box tucked in next to him. Sometimes Mick the Mouse would sleep inside the box, which they made cosy with some pieces of fluff pulled out of Evil Teddy (his father got in trouble for *that*, too).

One Saturday, SuperBaby's mother left SuperBaby with his father again, so that she could go shopping for shoes with Grandma.

'Look after the baby properly this time!' she scolded him. 'Don't let the cat into his room again!'

'But I didn't -'

'And don't hide his green teddy!' added Grandma.

'I never -'

'And he's sound asleep, so don't wake him up!' said the mother.

'I won't -'

'And don't put the green teddy in the fireplace again,' said Grandma.

'But I -'

The mother said, 'And listen outside his door every ten minutes to make sure he's not crying inside.'

'I will.'

'Lastly,' said Grandma, 'Put this in the bin.' She gave him a battered cereal box.

'Wait a minute,' said the father. 'This is baby's special box. He loves it.'

'It's dirty,' said Grandma. 'And it stinks! It smells like

a mouse has been living in it. *And* it's got bits of green teddy bear fluff inside!' She gave him a suspicious look.

'I didn't -' said the father.

'Ha!' said both the mother and Grandma. 'You did!'

So the father put the box in the bin, fed the cat, watched television... and fell asleep in his chair. Meanwhile, SuperBaby woke up and felt around for Ben the Box. He wanted to read the word Sugar again and practice the bigger words like Dicalcium Phosphate and Niacinamide.

Oh no! Ben the Box was missing! He began to cry, but no one heard him. So he climbed out of his cot and began searching the room. Still no box!

Cat the Cat scratched at the door, so SuperBaby flew to the doorknob and turned it to let the cat in.

'I've lost Ben the Box!' SuperBaby cried.

'Grandma took him out of your cot,' said Cat the Cat, sitting on Evil Teddy and cleaning a paw.

'Oh no!' exclaimed SuperBaby. 'He's been Box-napped!'

'Worse than that,' said the cat. 'They've put him in the rubbish bin on the drive.'

SuperBaby said, 'We must save him!'

'Good luck,' said the cat. 'That bin has a heavy lid.'

SuperBaby flew out the window and down to the bin. Cat the Cat was right: the big black bin had a heavy lid that kept banging shut as he tried to keep it open with one hand while poking about inside it with the other. Cat the Cat leapt onto the rim of the bin and held it open with her head so that the baby could fly down into the bin and search for Ben the Box.

Neither of them noticed the bin lorry stopping by the

house. Neither of them noticed a burly bin man walking up the drive.

'Hey – cat! – get outta there!' shouted the bin man. The cat fell off the bin; the bin lid clanged shut; inside, everything went dark.

Then SuperBaby was bounced about as the bin was rolled along the uneven drive. He tried to cry out, but he got a mouthful of apple peelings.

'Yummy!' he said.

Then the bin was turned upside down and he was falling, falling, falling… and soon he was underneath a big pile of stinky garbage that was being driven down the road inside a huge bin lorry.

He climbed up and sat on the top of the swaying pile of rubbish in the lorry. He thought about crying, then said bravely to himself, 'I must save Ben the Box!'

'Who?' asked a voice next to him.

SuperBaby peered into the garbage; two beady eyes peered out at him, above a furry nose and long whiskers. A long tail poked out nearby.

'I'm looking for Ben the Box,' said SuperBaby. 'Who are you? Are you a friend of Mick the Mouse?'

'Nah!' said the voice. 'I'm a rat. We don't hang out wiv mice. Sissies, they are.'

'What's your name?'

'Rocky.'

'Rocky the Rat!' said SuperBaby with delight. 'You can be my new friend!'

'Charmed, I'm sure,' said Rocky. 'But where's your Box friend gone?'

'I don't know,' said SuperBaby. 'They put Ben the Box in the bin. And now he's in *here* somewhere. And there's so much of everything here – I'll *never* find him!'

SuperBaby began to cry, just as any baby would do. Rocky the Rat crawled across and patted him kindly on the knee with a scratchy and rather dirty paw.

'There, there,' said the rat. 'Have some chips.'

He pulled forward a soggy bundle of crumpled newspaper and ripped it open to reveal a greasy bag of cold fried potatoes that smelled interesting: tangy and sweet and salty. SuperBaby tried one.

'They're wonderful!' he said and stopped crying immediately. 'I want to eat them forever!'

'Yeah,' said the rat. 'Nuffink like a bag of cold, greasy fries wiv salt an' vinegar. My favourite an' all.'

'There's so much nice food in the world!' exclaimed the baby. 'Have you tried baby food with rice and sugar and milk power and dicalcium phosphate in it?'

'Nah,' said the rat. 'Is it tasty?'

'It's as good as cold chips! It's yummy and sweet!'

'Wish I could try it,' said Rocky the Rat with a sigh.

'You can!' said the baby. 'If you help me find Ben the Box, you can come home with me and I'll share my cereal with you!'

'You got a deal,' said the rat.

'And when we find Ben the Box,' said the baby, 'I can fill him with chips! Hooray!'

'Good idea,' said Rocky. 'And I got me a plan…'

The bin lorry emptied its load at the Waste Centre and drove away. Rocky tunnelled his way out of the pile of rubbish, with SuperBaby following. Then he gave a sharp rat squeak and all his mates came running.

Soon, hundreds of rats were searching through the pile of rubbish, looking for a blue and red box about the size of a rat, with a picture of a happy baby on it. Ten minutes later, a delighted SuperBaby was hugging his box and Rocky the Rat was loading it with chips.

They flew back to the baby's house, SuperBaby holding the box under one arm and the rat under the other. He got into his cot and – being suddenly very tired – fell sound asleep.

When his mother came home shortly after this, she asked the father, 'Has the baby been okay?'

'Yes,' said his father. 'He hasn't made a sound.'

They went upstairs to check on the baby. There he was in his cot, hugging a box with one arm and something furry with the other.

'I told you to throw that box away!' said the mother.

'I did!'

'And what's he chewing on? I smell chips! Did you feed him chips?'

'I didn't!'

'But he's got some in his hand! And where did that rat toy come from? Have you hidden Green Teddy again?'

'But –'

'And his face is dirty! His hands too! Why can't you look after him properly? You're *so* in trouble this time!'

'But I –'

'Shh! You'll wake him!'

They tiptoed away, while the baby smiled in his sleep, dreaming of cold, greasy chips

Rick the Brick

You always remember your first toy, even if it's only a brick. SuperBaby had been taken to the park and placed on the lovely warm grass. He saw a ladybird being chased by a wasp and nearly flew off to save it, but stopped himself just in time. He pretended to be learning to crawl instead.

Meanwhile, his father had found an old red brick with lots of pretty moss on a top edge, like green hair. His father got a wax crayon from the toy bag and drew a face on the brick. He set it up on end: and it fell onto its face, making SuperBaby laugh. He set it up again: it fell onto its back. SuperBaby roared with laughter. Then his father made it fall sideways onto his mother's toes, which was even funnier - though his mother didn't think so.

SuperBaby insisted on taking Rick the Brick home with him. As they were walking out of the park, they passed the boy from next door, who was throwing sticks at the ducks in the river... Someone must save the ducks! This was a job for SuperBaby!

But he couldn't sneak away and save the ducks, because he was in the stroller. He thought about throwing Rick the Brick, but his parents would notice that... Aha! He had his dummy! He waited until they were near the river, then flung the dummy with all his might.

'Ouch!' the boy shouted as the dummy bounced off his head; but he kept throwing sticks.

SuperBaby pretended to cry; his parents stopped.

'He's lost his dummy,' said the father. He started searching on the ground around the stroller. Then the mother started searching as well. While they were busy, the baby felt about in the plastic bag his mother had put the dirty nappy in a few minutes ago... untaped it... threw it like a flying saucer....

'Aiiiiii! Help! Help!' screamed the boy as he ran home with another nappy on his head.

The Tale of "Bad the Burglar"

One day, SuperBaby heard his parents talking about robbers who break into people's houses at night and steal their special things. They called robbers like that *Burglars* and said they were bad.

There was something about it in the local newspaper,

so SuperBaby cried until they gave it to him. Then he read the article while tearing the pages to shreds.

The next morning at nap time, SuperBaby flew to the rubbish dump to collect Rocky the Rat, plus some chips to eat. Then he called his friends together.

'We must protect the house,' SuperBaby said. 'A burglar might come and steal Ben the Box!'

'And our cold, greasy fries,' said Rocky the Rat, pointing at the big bag of chips they were all eating from.

'My scratching tree,' said Cat the Cat.

'*Squeak!*' said Mick the Mouse.

'What did he say?' asked SuperBaby.

'He says the burglar might steal his tail,' said Rocky the Rat. 'That mouse is crazy.'

'We need some weapons,' the baby said. 'Can you find us some at that big place we were in? They had lots of scary things there.'

'You mean at the Waste Centre? Yeah, I'll go ask around tonight…'

Rocky returned at dawn with pineapple fritters, pickled onions, a water pistol and a pellet gun.

'These are great!' said SuperBaby, trying out the guns.

'Yes, but we'll have to find something to shoot out of them,' said Cat the Cat.

'Leave it to me!' said the baby.

The next few nights were difficult. SuperBaby tried to act as night watchman, but of course he kept falling asleep. Rocky the Rat and Cat the Cat had to take it in turn to watch, with Mick the Mouse as the runner to take *Squeak!* messages to SuperBaby if a burglar came.

And he did come. He was wearing a woolly hat pulled down to his eyebrows and was carrying a bag to put his loot in. He put a ladder up against the back of the house and climbed up it quietly to the open window. He put his head inside. No sound except the squeaking of a mouse. He smiled to himself.

'Hold it right there!' called a cute baby voice.

The burglar turned on his small flashlight. A baby was standing up in its cot, pointing two guns at him.

'I know who you are!' cried SuperBaby. 'You're Bad the Burglar, come to steal our treasure! Well, you can't have Ben the Box!'

'Or our chips and pickled onions,' said a rat-like voice from a dark corner.

'Or my scratching pole,' something meowed.

'*Squeak!*'

'He don't want your tail, you daft thing,' said Rocky.

'*Squeak! Squeak!*'

'Or your whiskers.'

The burglar laughed nastily. 'Heh heh... Those aren't real guns. That one's just a water gun! You can't scare me with *that*.'

'Yeah, but it's full of my wee,' said SuperBaby.

'Oh,' said the burglar, looking nervous.

The baby said, 'I've got a pellet gun too!'

'You have?' asked the burglar, looking even more nervous. 'What's in that?'

'Well, I've got poo from Rocky the Rat and Mick the Mouse, and bits from my nappy.'

There was a loud meow.

'Sorry – and I've got bits from Cat the Cat as well!'

The burglar said, 'That won't stop me! Heh heh...'

Still laughing quietly to himself, he started to climb over the window sill. The baby fired both guns.

'Yukkkkk!' cried the burglar, who really shouldn't

have been laughing nastily with his mouth open. He fell off the ladder and ran away.

But the next night he was back.

SuperBaby and his friends were waiting. The baby pointed his guns again and warned him to leave.

'It's serious this time, Bad the Burglar!' he shouted.

The burglar laughed nastily again. 'Look!' he said. 'I'm wearing a face mask and goggles. Why should I be scared of you this time? Heh heh heh....'

'I'll bite holes in your car tyres,' said a rat voice from behind the curtains.

'I'll dig up the flowers in your garden,' said a cat voice from below the window.

'*Squeak!*'

'And the mouse says he'll come round to your house and squeak at you in the middle of the night and wake you up. *Every single night.* It'll drive you nuts!'

The burglar said, 'I'm still not scared.'

Then Superbaby fired his guns.

'Oh yuk!' said the burglar. 'What's in those?'

'Baby sick!' laughed Superbaby. 'And there's plenty more where that came from!'

The burglar wiped his face mask and took out a gun of his own. A real gun.

'Back off, Baby!' he ordered.

'I've got lots of other friends to scare you with!' said SuperBaby, grabbing things and throwing them at the burglar. 'Here's Pam the ping pong ball... (*bop!*), Ted the toy tractor (*bink!*), Ollie the octopus (*bip!*).

The burglar laughed cruelly as well as nastily. 'Heh heh! You'll have to do better than that, Baby! I'm coming inside!' He began to climb through the window.

'Here's another friend,' said SuperBaby. 'Meet Rick the Brick! Get his toes, Rick!'

Whack!

The brick hit the burglar on his head, knocking him out the window and all the way to the ground.

Bad the Burglar was so scared that he gave up being a burglar and became an investment banker instead.

A very special ending

When SuperBaby was a year old, he decided to let his parents know he could talk: so he started using little words like Cat and Brick and Cold greasy chips.

However, it was sometimes difficult to stop himself from saying too much. Just when he thought life was settling down, his mother said to him:

'Guess what? In five months' time, you're going to have a little brother or sister!'

'Oh,' said SuperBaby. 'I thought you were just getting

fat from eating too many chips!'

'What?' asked his mother.

'*Oops,*' said SuperBaby. 'Cat brick cold greasy chips yum yum!'

'Awww,' said his mother. 'You're getting very good at talking, aren't you?'

SuperBaby shared the news with his friends.

'What shall we call it?' he asked. 'Bob the Baby?'

'It might be a girl,' said Rocky.

'No!' said SuperBaby. 'That's too scary!'

'Girls are great,' said Cat the Cat. 'She can be Bella the Baby.'

'*Squeak!*'

'Nah, Mick: she won't have a tail.'

SuperBaby said, 'Are girl babies nice to play with?'

'They're lots of fun.'

'Just as fun as boy babies.'

'*Squeak!*'

'Mick the Mouse says we need to start collecting toys for the new baby.'

'Hooray! We'll get Sid the snake -'

'Stan the stick -'

'Simon the slug and Sarah the snail -'

'Sally the stone!'

'Yay! We'll hide them at the back of the wardrobe. We've only got five months to go! We'll fill that wardrobe to the top! What fun we'll have!'

And they did.

The Ten Wishes

The voices

The Fairy has a fine musical voice like a tinkling bell. It's full of fun and sunlight. She sings like a happy bird – well, a happy bird bobbing its head to a heavy bass rhythm. When she's listening to her music, she talks to Billy in that vague, half-aware manner used by your parents when they're busy with something else.

Billy sounds friendly, kind and patient. You can tell he likes pretty much everything and everybody (even Thug the bully). You can imagine him talking kindly to alligators and eccentric bicycles. He's the sort of person who sometimes gets ignored because he doesn't say very much: but he's the best friend ever.

His Mother is puzzled at all times and a bit exasperated about life. You can understand that: not many people have had to put up with a husband being eaten by arctic wolves, alligators in the garden and the house suddenly turning blue.

The Three Evil Aunts have a certain gooselike honking, hissing and cackling quality to their voices. They look at Billy the way geese look at a tasty slug, eyes all dark and glittery, voices all pretended kindness, diamond bracelets jangling.

The Witches sometimes sound scary; sometimes lovely. It's hard to tell a witch by the voice. But there's a little something in the way they say things that sends a nasty chill up your spine and down into your liver, spleen, kidneys, appendix and kneecaps.

The Gators sound friendly in a chomping sort of way. They'll probably bite your leg off, but they'll apologise for it afterwards. You should always carry peanut butter toast with you in Florida, in case you meet one of these. I do.

The story

In memory of Mark Glover, August 2011 - who reminded me about this story

Once there was a boy named Billy who caught a fairy by mistake. He was trying to catch a tennis ball, but he was useless at all ball games: so the ball bounced off his head... he fell to the ground... and got up with a fairy in his hand instead of the ball.

He didn't know this and was just about to throw the fairy when a small, clear voice scolded him:

'Stop squeezing me! I'm not a sponge!'

Billy opened his hand slowly. He was holding a small, elegant creature with wings, long multicoloured hair and a rather bent wand. She whacked him on the thumb with the wand; and he dropped her.

'Nooooo! - Don't do that, either! - *Ouch!*' she shouted as she fell, landing on his right shoe. She whacked his shoe with her wand, too. It was even more bent now.

'Sorry.' He picked up the ball, which he threw back to his friend – well, almost. It bounced off a dinner lady's broad backside and broke a classroom window.

Billy groaned. 'I wish I hadn't done that,' he said.

'That won't work,' the fairy called up to him from her perch on his right shoe. 'That's an impossible wish. You can't change the past. Try again.'

'What?' asked Billy. 'You mean I can have a wish?'

She was suddenly sitting on his left shoulder. 'You caught me. You get ten.'

'Wow! Can you mend the window?'

'Done,' said the fairy, snapping her fingers towards the building. 'Nine left.'

Billy looked across at the window. It was perfect again.

'That's amazing!' he said.

'No I'm not. I'm perfectly normal. All fairies are. Only humans are crazy.'

'I didn't say you were crazy. I said *amazing.*'

'No you didn't,' she said crossly. 'You humans mumble your words dreadfully, but I can tell the difference between crazy and lazy. I'm *not* lazy, by the way.'

'I didn't -'

'Did! You're just making it worse by denying it.'

Billy looked at her more closely. There was some sort of plug in each of her ears, with wires coming out from them. 'You're wearing a hearing aid!' he exclaimed.

'Nonsense,' she said. She pulled the plug from one ear and stuck it into Billy's ear instead. A loud, thumping music nearly blew a hole in his head.

'Troll Rock,' she said. 'Good, isn't it?'

'It's horrible!' groaned Billy.

'Glad you agree. *Adorable.* But I don't recommend you go to their music concerts. Even the rocks start vibrating and that ruins your hearing, I'm told. Fortunately, mine hasn't been affected.'

'I think you're wrong there,' said Billy.

'That's sweet of you. I just had it coloured.' She smiled at him and fluffed up her long blond hair – streaked with green and blue and red and purple and – well, just about every colour Billy knew the name of. 'Now, what would you like for your other nine wishes?'

'I have to go back to class now,' he said. 'Please can I tell you after school?'

'Yes, you can. Eight wishes left now.' She clicked her fingers at him.

'What? That wasn't a wish!'

'Oh yes it was!' She smiled at him triumphantly and disappeared.

Colourful wishes

As he was walking home from school that afternoon, the fairy appeared again, sitting on his right shoulder this time. 'Thought of your wishes yet?' she asked.

'Not properly,' he said. 'But I know I definitely want a new bike.'

'Easy,' she said, clicking her toes this time. 'Seven left!'

Billy was now riding a blue bicycle. An *old* blue bicycle, with pedals that clonked and a front mudguard that wobbled.

'This isn't what I wanted!' he shouted.

'Then you shouldn't have asked for it!' retorted the fairy, who was riding on the handlebars facing forward, with her long multi-streaked hair flowing behind her in the wind. 'This was the nearest blue bike I could find.'

'*New*, not blue,' said Billy. 'And – wait a minute – this bike looks just like the one that -'

'Hey!' shouted Thug the school bully, who was running alongside him now. 'Get off my bike!'

After a few minutes of heated argument, Billy picked himself up from the ground and started walking home.

'That boy was very rude,' said the fairy from his shoulder.

'Well, it *was* his bike,' said Billy. 'You shouldn't have given me someone else's bicycle.'

'You didn't tell me not to,' said the fairy stubbornly. 'You just said a blue bike.'

'Not a blue bike. A *new* bike. I want my wish back. Or a replacement bike.'

'Whatever!' She turned up the volume on her music player so loud that Billy's head began to vibrate. He had to shout to make himself heard:

'I've thought of another wish!'

She shook her head. 'You can't ride fish. They don't have wheels.'

He carefully pulled the earphones from her ears.

'Oooooh,' she said. 'Isn't it quiet here?'

'Listen,' he said. 'My mum's always complaining that the house is too small and everything needs repainting. So I thought maybe I could ask for a new house, twice the size of our old one, with a new fence around it and a big green gate – or maybe a red one.'

'You do ask for some odd things,' said the fairy. 'And that's too many colours. But I'll give you one of each. That's three wishes. Only four left now!'

'No!' said Billy. 'It's only one wish. The new house, with a green gate or –'

'Just joking! Six left!' laughed the fairy and disappeared again as she clicked her fingers.

Gators

Billy walked on until he came to the gate that led into

his small front yard. He sighed. The ancient fence had simply turned blue and the rickety old gate was still a dirty white. He pushed it open and stepped inside.

Then he jumped back outside because something big and green had snapped at his left leg.

He peered through the bars of the gate. A large green alligator looked back at him.

'Hello,' said Billy.

'Hi,' said the green alligator.

'Hi,' said another voice, to the right of the gate: a red alligator this time.

'Can I come in?' Billy asked.

'Can I bite yer leg?'

'Can I bite yer udder leg?'

Billy said, 'No, you can't.'

'Den you can't come in.'

'No way.'

Billy insisted, 'But it's my house.'

'So?'

'So? We's in charge now.'

'I didn't ask for you. I asked for a green gate, or -'

'Dat's me. A green gator.'

'Oh. Or a red one.'

'Yeah, dat's me.'

'Oh.' Billy thought hard. 'So you're *my* gators. That means you have to do what I tell you.'

'No, we don't.'

'Dat's right, we don't.'

'If you don't do what I say, I'll wish for you to disappear! Or – or I'll wish you very, very small. So small that everyone laughs at you.'

The two gators looked at each other.

'Dat wouldn't be fair.'

'No way. I'm not havin' people laugh at me.'

Billy said, 'You'll have to stay out of sight, then. Live in the bushes or something. And don't bite anyone.'

The gators whispered for a while, then nodded.

'But we gotta have breakfast each morning.'

'Yeah, a piece of toast each.'

'Wid peanut butter on it.'

'Loadsa peanut butter.'

Billy's house was now a bright blue colour from top to bottom. Even the glass in the windows was blue. But the house seemed to be the same size as before.

Inside, all the wallpaper was now also blue. His mother was trying to wash the blue off the windows.

'What have you been up to?' she asked accusingly. 'Did you do this? Or has your grandfather been messing about with his paint sprayer again?'

Billy said, 'It was a fairy. I caught her and -'

'Billy, this isn't funny. The windows are ruined, and you're making up stories? Go to your room! *Fairies, indeed!* Fairies don't do decorating. They – wait a minute! Maybe it's one of those television house makeover things. Well, that would be nice. Shame they didn't make the house bigger while they were at it.'

Billy was about to go up the staircase to his room. But he stopped. 'Mum!' he called. 'Something's gone wrong with the stairs!'

The stairs used to go up. Now they went down as well. Downstairs - underground - there was a big playroom, a study and an extra bedroom, each of them a different shade of blue. And at the end of the playroom was a large glass tank built into the wall – a blue tank filled with blue water and two alligators, a green one and a red one. The gators waved a paw each.

'That's amazing!' said his mother.

'It's crazy,' said Billy.

'I'm **not** lazy!' whispered an angry voice in his ear…

Three evil aunts

It should have been a happy day after that: after all, they had half a new house to explore. But Billy's three evil aunts came to tea without warning.

His evil aunts were tall and thin, with long, stringy necks and an evil glint in every eye. They were his father's scary sisters, and ever since his father had been eaten by wolves in the snowy arctic wilderness, his aunts had been trying to take Billy away from his mother. They didn't have any children of their own and thought Billy would be better off with them instead of his kind, sweet mother. Besides, they wanted someone to do the washing up, mopping and dusting: someone cheap and easy to boss around, like a child. They were in fact rather rich but they didn't like spending money – except on fashion accessories.

They were stalking around the garden now in glittery shoes, clutching their matching designer handbags and smiling scarily at Billy as he showed them the carrots and beans and potatoes on one side of the path, with foxgloves, forget-me-nots and hollyhocks on the other.

A couple of large shapes were lurking in the bushes, so he didn't take his aunts there. He noticed that the bushes seemed to have spread a little, as if the garden was expanding wherever the alligators went.

The aunts' diamond bracelets sparkled in the sun and the tiny pink flamingo feathers in their small, bejewelled black hats were ruffled by a gentle breeze. They were smirking to one another and whispering as they followed Billy.

'Shall I tell him now?' asked Aunt One.

'I want to do it!' said Aunt Two.

'No, *I'll* tell him!' insisted Aunt Three. 'Little Billy: in two days' time, you'll be *our* little boy. Ha ha! As soon as we go home and sign some nasty pieces of paper, the police will come and take you away from your useless mother and give you to *us* instead.'

Aunt One added, 'That will be so much better for you! We'll make you do three hours homework every day!'

'– Four hours at weekends! Think how clever you'll become!'

'We'll give you lots of good chores to make you strong, like washing dishes –'

'- ironing!'

'- dusting!'

'- cleaning the toilets twice a day!'

'- pooooooeeeee!'

'- washing our silk nighties by hand!'

'- and our Gucci socks!'

'- pooooooeeeee!'

'- and lots of other chores that are GOOD for little children to do!'

Billy said, 'But I like it here. And I like my mum.'

'- No you don't!'

'- You don't have enough money to be happy!'

'- Your house is too small!'

Billy said, 'We've had it extended.'

The three aunts craned their skinny necks around and looked back at the house. They made disapproving, honking sounds, like unhappy geese.

'- You're imagining things!'

'- You read too many *Wicked Tales* books!'

'- You've been brainwashed!'

The three aunts turned their heads back around and smiled at Billy, then said in chorus: 'You're going to be *our* little boy!'

Billy said, 'I wish you would -' But he stopped himself.

'What?' asked three voices together.

Then a fourth voice he knew well by now added, 'I didn't catch that wish. What did you ask for?'

'I didn't finish it,' said Billy, talking to his left shoulder. But the fairy wasn't there. 'I didn't,' he repeated to the right.

Six suspicious eyes stared at him.

'You've gone crackers!' said Aunt One.

'You're potty!' said Aunt Two.

'Crazy as a loon!' said Aunt Three.

'No I'm not,' said Billy. 'I was talking to a – a friend of mine. She's around here somewhere. She – *There* you are!' he said to Aunt One's little black hat. The fairy was standing on it and trying to pull one of the pink feathers out of the brim. She had done her hair differently this time: it was twisted and woven to make it look like two long horns sticking out on either side of her head.

'Are you talking to my hat, young man?' asked Aunt One. 'That's very rude!' She took the hat off and dropped it into her handbag, which she clipped shut.

A little voice came from the bag: 'Let me out!'

'Ooooh your handbag is talking!' said Aunt Two.

'You ought to take it back to the shop,' said Aunt Three. 'It shouldn't do that.'

The fairy shouted through the crack in the bag, 'I'll give you a wish if you let me out!'

'A wishing handbag!' said Aunt One.

'A wishbag!'

'Ooooh how lovely! What should we wish for?'

'A nice cup of tea and some scones!'

'No – a million pounds!'

'A billion!'

'A zillion!'

'*And* a nice cup of tea.'

'We could wish for the winning lottery numbers.'

'And the right bingo cards!'

'Or maybe we could fly!'

'Yes, like birds! Then we could go on holiday without paying for airplanes!'

Aunt One said, 'We mustn't rush. Let's go home and make a list first.'

'I can't wait!

'I wish we were -'

'Don't say it!'

'Oooooh I nearly wished we were home already.'

'That would be silly. *I* wish we could fly – just like those geese up there – but I'm not going to wish *that*.'

'You just did.'

'Oooops!'

As Billy watched, his three evil aunts changed into geese, two of them wearing bejewelled black hats with pink feathers in the brim. They all hissed at Billy, curving their necks around and glaring at him with their angry black eyes. They chased him around the lawn a few times and cornered him by the old, wobbly blue fence. They stalked closer, closer, their hissing bills snaking towards the trapped boy; then a couple of sleepy alligators wandered up.

'Where's my toast and peanut butter?

'Yeah, and mine. Hey – geese!'

'Dey'll do! Tasty, geese is.'

'Snack time!'

The alligators chased the geese around the lawn, with Billy following. The geese flapped and waddled very quickly, heading for their handbags; Billy ran ahead and snatched up Aunt One's bag just in time. He tried to open it, but a hissing goose bill snatched the bag from his hands and flew away with it. The two other geese also rose into the air and they all sailed away, honking angrily, until they disappeared from sight.

'The poor fairy,' said Billy. 'She's stuck with my evil aunts!'

'Poor fairy,' agreed the green gator.

'I didn't see no ants,' said the red one. 'Just geese.'

'Silly boy,' said another voice. 'Did you really think I could be trapped for long in a *handbag*?'

The fairy was sitting on his left shoulder again. She reached into her pocket and took out a little knife. 'That bag's got a hole in it now!' she laughed. She put the knife away and waved a pink feather at Billy. 'Got it!' she said proudly.

'My aunts -' began Billy.

'I don't see any aunts,' said the fairy.

'No ants,' agreed the red gator. 'No toast neither.'

'Just geese. Widout peanut butter on 'em.'

Billy insisted to the fairy, 'They shouldn't be geese. You'll have to turn them back.'

The fairy asked, 'Black geese? That would be weird.'

'I mean I wish they were *back* to being human.'

'No. Can't do it. Wish Wars aren't allowed.'

'But -'

'They wished it for themselves, so it can't be changed by *you*.' She stuck her tongue out at Billy, then disappeared.

A variety of bikes

'Any more wishes?' the fairy asked after supper. She was seated on Billy's chest of drawers, leaning back against Ben the Teddy. Her earplugs were in and she was nodding her tiny head to some nameless thumping music. Poor Ben the Teddy seemed to be wincing at each note.

'I still want my bicycle – but wait a moment.'

The fairy looked at her watch. 'A moment's up!' she called cheerily.

'I meant: wait until I explain exactly what I want.' He brought out a store catalogue and showed the fairy the bicycle he wanted. 'One like this,' he said.

'Hmmm,' said the fairy. 'Easy peasy lemon squeezy!' She clicked her fingers at the picture and disappeared.

In her place was a tiny bicycle made out of paper.

'What's the use of that?' shouted Billy. But there was no reply.

'Maybe she doesn't work after six o'clock,' he said.

The next morning, she reappeared at breakfast, next to his cereal bowl. She stood on tiptoe and reached into the bowl for a honey-coated oat puff, which she ate happily, sitting on the table and humming to herself.

Billy's mother was in the next room. He whispered to the fairy, 'I meant a *real* bike. Like the bicycle in the picture, but real.'

The fairy nodded her head. 'I can do that.' She prepared to snap her fingers; Billy stopped her.

He said slowly and clearly, 'Just to make it plain: I want a bicycle the same make and model as the one in the picture. The right size for me to ride on. Please.'

'You don't have to shout! I'm not deaf, you know.' She clicked her fingers and... a small rug appeared next to the breakfast table.

'That's not a bicycle,' Billy observed.

'I don't know how to make a bicycle,' the fairy replied grumpily. 'You can ride on this magic carpet instead.' The rug rose into the air and tried to fly out through the open window. It miscalculated and bumped into the wall below the window. It backed up and tried again. This time it bumped into the wall to the right of the window. Finally it flew out, nearly knocking over a vase of flowers on the window sill.

'No,' said Billy.

'So grouchy! Try this, then.' She clicked her fingers twice again and the rug grew into a pony, which stuck its head back in through the window. It started to eat the flowers from the vase.

'No!' said Billy again. 'Everyone would laugh at me if I rode a pony to school.'

The fairy clicked her fingers again and the pony trotted away. Then the two alligators stuck their snouts above the window ledge and ate the rest of the flowers.

'You can ride me to school,' said the green one. 'The first kid what laughs at you loses a leg.'

'Yeah. Chomp, scream, chomp, scream.
Dat'll teach 'em!' said the red one.

'No!' insisted Billy. 'I'm not riding an
alligator to school! I want a bicycle!'

The fairy stamped her foot. 'You're
so annoying!' she complained.

'And you're usel- ' Billy stopped himself.

'What?' she asked in a threatening tone. 'You're mumbling again!'

'I want a bicycle. *Please.*'

Click! 'I've done my best. It's outside waiting for you.
And you've used half your wishes.'

Billy cycled to school that morning on a bicycle with
wheels that weren't quite round. Its pedals clicked and
clomped as if it was a pony trotting along the road, and
its bell made a whinnying noise.

Billy kept his mouth firmly shut as he cycled, to stop
himself wishing that the bicycle was better: he mustn't
waste any more wishes. He didn't even say anything
when Thug the school bully threw a tomato at him. The
thought came into his head '*I wish YOU were a tomato!*':
but he didn't say it.

It was a very odd bicycle. Besides its up and down
motion (which made him feel like he was on a trotting
horse), it sometimes jumped over small obstacles like
sticks on the road or potholes. And if he leaned back,
the bike would rise in the air and glide above the
ground, though it tended to bump into kerbs or trees
when it did this.

It also had a bad habit of stopping when they came to
large clumps of grass and sticking its front wheel into
the grass, making little chomping sounds.

Thug came up as Billy parked the bike in the school rack. 'That's a stupid bike!' he sneered, giving its rear wheel a kick. Then he fell over.

'It kicked me!' he groaned. 'Your bike kicked me!'

'Sorry,' said Billy. 'But you kicked it first.'

Thug got up. He went to the front of the bike instead and reached for the handlebars.

'I wouldn't do that,' warned Billy. 'I think that end of the bike probably -'

'Owwwwww!' shouted Thug.

'- bites,' said Billy.

Happy hoppy teacher

His teacher Mr Crabby shouted at Billy for being two seconds late into the classroom. He was in a bad mood. Actually, he'd been in a bad mood for twenty years but today was his worst mood ever.

'Mr Crabby's being really mean today,' whispered a friend as they were doing some additions. 'I hate him!'

Billy was a kind child and found himself saying, 'He's all right really. Sometimes he's happy and funny. I just wish he was always like that.'

Then he put his hand over his mouth, because there was a snapping of fingers – and a sudden disappearance of Mr Crabby.

A quiet voice from beside his pencil case said, 'You do have some odd wishes! But you're right: it really suits him. By the way, only four wishes left now!'

'What suits him?' asked Billy. But the fairy had gone; and Billy began to worry.

The whole class was worried now. Mr Crabby wasn't there. In his place, a very happy – and hoppy - blue bunny was dancing about. It had a blue necktie about

its neck and blue glasses dangling on
one ear (both of which soon fell off).

Someone ran to tell the office, leaving the door open. The blue bunny
twitched his nose twice and was out
of the class in a moment. They all chased after him, up
and down the corridors, through the library, through
the hall (interrupting a choir rehearsal) through the music room and out onto the playground.

The Mr Crabby bunny was very fast; and he seemed
determined to taunt his pursuers. He would run about
twenty metres, pause and pretend to nibble grass while
the children crept up on him; then he would leap into
the air and run twenty metres in a different direction.

'We need some dogs to chase him,' said someone.

'No! They might hurt him!' said another.

A third student said, 'I wish *we* were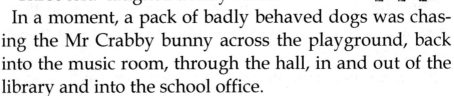
dogs. We'd catch him quickly then.'

'Yeah, wish we were dogs!'

'Me too!'

Billy said, 'Me too. Oops...'

'Three left!' laughed a fairy voice.

In a moment, a pack of badly behaved dogs was chasing the Mr Crabby bunny across the playground, back
into the music room, through the hall, in and out of the
library and into the school office.

The school secretary pulled out a big gun. The dogs
and bunny slid to a halt and ran out again. But some of
them were wet now, because it was a water gun. The
bunny escaped through another exit onto the playground, pursued by most of the dogs.

As Billy ran barking along the corridor, he saw the
Headteacher about to walk into the classroom. She was

opening the door; it was too late to stop her; she would see that the whole class had run off!

'I wish we were back in there!' he called in a growly puppy voice.

'Two left!' said a voice from somewhere on his back.

The Headteacher stopped in the doorway. She was staring into a classroom of puppies being taught by a blue rabbit. The rabbit was reading from a book (*Mmmff crvmff dppbhfmf!*) and the puppies were scribbling something onto pieces of paper, their little tongues hanging out and some of them scratching at fleas with their rear paws as they wrote with their front ones.

'Oh. Sorry. Wrong… room,' the Headteacher said. Then she went back to her office to lie down.

As soon as the Headteacher shut the door, the bunny dropped the book he'd been trying to hold in his bunny paws. The dogs let go of their pencils. Dogs and bunny watched each other, each waiting for the other to move first. The Mr Crabby bunny wrinkled his nose again, leaped onto a table and sprang out through an open window. The dogs barked excitedly and joined him.

They raced through the playground again, crawled under a fence and began charging about in a small wood full of nettles and brambles.

But the bunny had escaped. And Billy realised that most of the parents would be upset to find that their children were now dogs - even Thug's parents. There was Thug the Dog now, chasing a squirrel. The squirrel leapt for the safety of a tree – Thug leapt – the squirrel was trapped between Thug the Dog's jaws –

'I wish we were children again.'

Thug was now a boy with a squirrel in his mouth. The other children were staring at him. The squirrel was staring at him, too. The squirrel was puzzled. The squirrel was annoyed. The squirrel bit Thug on the nose!

'Owwwwwww!' A crying Thug ran back to school.

The other children crawled out of the nettles, brambles and mud. They went back to their class and tried to finish the last piece of work ever set by Mr Crabby.

Final wish

'Last wish!' announced the Fairy on Thursday. 'And you'd better choose it today because I'm going to spend tomorrow getting dressed and made up for a Troll Rock concert.' Humming to herself, she started dancing and spinning round on top of Billy's bookshelf, knocking over the dusty birthday cards from three months ago.

Billy smiled. He'd had the best idea ever. 'My final wish is to have another ten wishes,' he announced.

The fairy fell over and lay on her back looking at the

ceiling. She groaned, 'I'm soooooo dizzy now… Ten of them? That's a lot. Are you sure that's what you want?'

'Yes!' said Billy stubbornly.

'You do ask for some odd things,' the fairy said with a sigh. 'It'll take me a while to get that many together. But I can have them ready for you tomorrow morning. Are you sure -'

'Yes!'

'All right. Don't say I didn't warn you…'

The next morning (which was Friday), Billy was ready for school super-early. Ten more wishes! He could hardly wait to get started.

He wheeled his pony bike to the gate, fed the alligators two slices of peanut butter toast each, and set off on the road to school.

'Ten wishes!' he said to himself as he pedalled. *Clompity clomp clippity clop whinny whinny whinny.*

Another bicycle drew up beside him. An incredibly scary-looking woman with a tall pointy hat turned and smiled at him. 'HELLO, BILLY!' she cackled. She gave him a big wink, then cycled away.

There was something very wrong with her bicycle. Its wheels were spinning backwards. And in the place of a crossbar and a proper seat, it had a broom handle with an old-fashioned broom on the end.

While Billy was still wondering about this, he turned a corner and nearly ran over a man who was so raggedy that he looked like a scarecrow… a scarecrow on roller blades. Only, the roller blades didn't quite reach the ground.

'HEY THERE, BILLY,' the scarecrow man called in a thin, muffled voice – a voice of straw and sawdust. He seemed to have a scarecrow head as well, with a face of lumpy cloth that had eyes painted on.

Billy cycled past him as fast as possible, glided over a few bumps and puddles and stopped at some traffic lights. A large black car drew up next to him. Its window opened with an electric hum.

'Hi, Billy,' said a soft voice. She had blond hair, lovely eyes and flashing teeth. Her beautiful hands weren't touching the steering wheel – she was brushing her hair and sending text messages on her phone at the same time – and yet when the lights changed, the car still managed to turn left all by itself. Billy watched her go; she kept looking at him, and her head turned slowly in a circle until it faced backwards as she kept her eyes on him while driving away.

Another six weird people called to him on the way to school. That made nine in total. And as he walked into the classroom, he saw number ten hobbling towards him, calling out:

'HELLO, BILLY! GOOD TO SEE YOU! I'M YOUR NEW TEACHER!'

Ten witches. That's what the fairy had given him. Ten horrible witches.

The new teacher seemed to be a woman, but she might have been a man wearing a long black dress. She (or he) was very tall and very thin, with long white hair that fell to her waist. She wrote her name on the board: it started with Mrzhvtsk and had about twenty letters in it, most of them consonants. When she turned to face the class, one of her eyes fell out and bounced about on her desk. She caught it and popped it back into place. The children all screamed.

'WE'RE GOING TO HAVE SUCH FUN!' she cackled. Then the other eye popped out and she had to put that one back as well. More screaming.

She took a stick out of her big black bag and whacked the desk with it.

'STOP THAT NOISE!' she commanded. The class fell silent immediately. Then she snatched books from her bag and threw them across the room. Each book landed perfectly in the middle of a child's desk.

'EVERYBODY WILL TURN TO PAGE THIRTEEN AND WRITE OUT WHAT'S WRITTEN ON IT, BACKWARDS. NOW!'

One child put his hand up.

'NO!' she shouted. She pointed her stick, and the hand slapped the top of the child's own head.

It was the scariest school day ever. Not only did her eyes keep falling out, but one of her arms fell off just before lunchtime and she had to fasten it back on with a screwdriver from her black bag.

Then both ears slipped down around her dress collar: so she hauled them up, got out the classroom stapler and stapled each ear into place.

As the children filed out of the class to go home that afternoon, she waved merrily and promised, 'MORE FUN ON MONDAY!' Then she added, 'THANKS FOR INVITING ME, BILLY!'

Everyone turned to look at Billy.

'I didn't,' he said.

They continued to look at Billy. He promised, 'I'll make sure she doesn't come back.'

'Please do that,' said Thug, who was as scared as anyone. 'I'll be your friend forever!'

'Wow! That's a deal,' said Billy.

He cycled home as fast as his pony carpet cycle would go, ignoring all the odd, scary people who called to him as he passed. He slammed the gate behind him and said to the waiting gators, 'Don't let anyone in!'

'Not even you?'

'Not even us?'

'You know what I mean!'

'We does?'

'Nah, we doesn't.'

Billy explained, 'Keep eve-ryone out except you two and me – and my mum.'

'And if someone gets in, do we keep 'em in?'

'Or if dey's already in, do we bite 'em?'

'If they're in, just – oh, I'll explain later. I need to talk to the fairy now.'

'Is she in? Or out?'

'Can we bite her?'

Billy wheeled the bike to the house, shouting, 'Fairy! I need to talk to you! Fairy!'

His mother opened the door and looked out. 'Are you all right?' she asked. 'You don't look well.'

'I had a bad day at school. Fairy! Fairy!'

His mother said, 'Stop shouting! People will think you've gone crazy. Come inside and have your supper.'

As he ate, Billy thought hard. The fairy wasn't coming back, because he'd used up his ten wishes. And she'd said something about going out to a concert. Maybe...

He asked his mother, 'Is there a rock concert in town tonight?'

'How should I know?' she asked, puzzled.

'How can I find out?' he asked.

'Internet, of course. But why -'

Billy was gone to the computer like a shot. But he couldn't find anything about a rock concert nearby. Oh well...

Party party

As he was trying to fall asleep, he imagined the fairy flying far away to some big field where thousands of people were listening to heavy, thumping music. He could almost hear it: *bahdah-bahda badhummm bah-dah-bahdah badhummm-dhummm-dhummm*.

He *could* hear it! He sat up. It was Troll Rock! He recognised one of the tracks from the fairy's music player!

He opened his window and leaned out. Somewhere out there – not too far away – a band was playing in the darkness, its guitars and drums and other instruments making the whole house vibrate.

He dressed and crept out of the house, pushing his bicycle down the path as quietly as possible. He got to the gate and reached for the latch.

'Nah, can't let you do dat.'

'Gonna havta bite yer leg off.'

'Bofe legs.'

'But it's me! Billy!'

Two dark shadows looked up at him doubtfully.

'You doesn't look like him.'

'He ain't as black as you is.'

Billy said, 'It's dark out here, you daft gators. Look!' He turned the bike light on himself.

'Oh yeah.'

'Got any toast?'

'I'll bring you some tomorrow. Must go now.'

He cycled warily through darkened streets, trying to follow the music. Finally he came upon a big football stadium with lots of cars parked outside it and an enormous thumping, throbbing music coming from inside. He cycled up to the entrance gate.

The men at the gate laughed at him.

'Too young, sonny,' said one. 'Gotta be fifteen. Got your ID on you?'

Another said, 'And it'll cost you forty to get in. Brought some cash, have you?'

Billy shook his head sadly.

'Go home then,' they said.

'Yeah, unless your little bike can jump fences!'

Billy looked at the fence. It was about three metres high, maybe more. He sighed, turned his bike around and cycled away.

The men laughed at him as he went. They stopped laughing when – fifty metres out - he swung the bike in a wide circle and charged at the fence, picking up speed with every sweep of the pedals. Faster he went, and faster. The men were shouting at him now, but he didn't even glance at them. He pushed even harder on the pedals. The bike was storming along now. *Clompity clomp clippity clop whinny! Clompity clomp clippity clop whinny whinny whinny!*

He was twenty metres from the wall… fifteen… he leaned back and pulled the handlebars upward. The bike leapt into the air. And still he pedalled, and still it accelerated, and still it rose. Not quite high enough: it hit the wall halfway up; but then he cycled straight up the wall and teetered on the very top for a moment before cycling down the other side.

He parked the bike behind some vans and went in search of the fairy. But it was hopeless. There were thousands of people in here. And it was dark. And she was tiny. And she couldn't possibly hear him if he called her.

Just a moment! She would be wherever the noise was

loudest! He fought his way through the crowd to the front of the stage and watched the musicians leaping around, sending notes crashing through the loudspeakers… The loudspeakers! He ran from one set of speakers to another, peering through the darkness. Not here. Not here, either. Not – ah!

There was a tiny figure dressed in glittery clothes, spinning about in front of an enormous bank of booming loudspeakers. She leaped and dived and swayed, did a couple of somersaults, then began dancing and skipping in some wild fairy salsa routine.

The noise here was so loud that Billy's whole body was throbbing with it. But he pushed forward through the crowd, climbed the barrier and leaped onto the stage. One of the security guard tried to catch him but he dodged away and dived upon the fairy. It was the best bit of fielding he'd ever done: he snatched her up, put her in his pocket and leaped off the stage into the dancing, singing crowd, the way he'd seen others doing: crowd-surfing. Fortunately, the crowd caught him.

When he got back to his bicycle, he took the fairy out of his pocket and shouted (it was still very noisy, even behind the vans), 'Fairy, it's me! Billy!'

She pouted up at him. 'Let me go! I want to dance!'

'Not yet,' said Billy. 'You have to cancel my last wish. It wasn't what I wanted. Not *witches*. Send them back. Undo the wish!'

'Can't undo wishes!' said the fairy grumpily.

'But please,' said Billy. 'It's horrible. You've got to.'

'No, I don't.'

'Pretty please?'

The fairy smiled at him. 'Do you like my hair?' she asked. It was standing up in multi-coloured spikes all over, each spike about a fairy hand's length long.

'It's great,' said Billy. 'And your clothes are amazing. Please will you undo the wish?'

She shook her head. 'Can't. *Won't!* But you did catch me again, didn't you? On purpose this time, too.'

'Yeah,' said Billy. 'So -'

'Ten more wishes, and the first can send the witches back. But now *go away*! I need to do some dancing!'

She clicked her fingers and was gone.

Billy wheeled his bicycle to the main gate, where the men let him out. 'Great bike, kid,' they said respectfully. He cycled home slowly, persuaded the gators to let him back through the gate, then climbed into bed and slept peacefully.

Final wishes again?

The next morning, he opened his sock drawer to find a snoring fairy in it, her body pushed down into one of his softest, furriest socks. She opened her eyes and tried to focus on him.

'Had a great night,' she groaned, turned over and went to sleep again. He pulled the sock up so that she looked cosy; then he shut the drawer halfway.

Billy was wandering around the garden after lunch when she appeared on his shoulder, looking much fresher. 'I expect you'll want to undo all the spells and start over?' she asked him.

He looked around at the garden, which seemed to have grown even larger. He looked back at the house, seeing the blue windows sparkle in the sunlight. Two long faces – one red, one green – poked out of the undergrowth and smiled at him. Beyond them, his odd blue bicycle was grazing on the lawn.

'I think everything is perfect just the way it is,' he said.

Trog the Thunderdog

The voices

Trog the Thunderdog used to be a small brownish mutt who chased sticks for the witch. Now he's a big brownish mutt who chases lightning bolts. He has a booming bark and a gravelly growl and a warm, wicked woof. What he wants most of all is for people to pat him on the head and call him a Good Dog.

The **Littlest Thundertroll** thinks very slowly. He talks the way he thinks, as if he's building each sentence out of a handful of rocks. He's a gentle, good-natured, amusing, square-shaped greenish creature who gets into all sorts of trouble by accident. **All trolls** sound a bit gruff, rough and tough - even small ones.

The **King of the Thundertrolls** is a jolly green giant who speaks with a posh accent. He's like one of those distant uncles you meet at family weddings, who pats you on the head and talks at you very loudly, as if you're deaf. His first words are usually "Goodness! Haven't you grown!"

The **Queen of the Thundertrolls** talks down to all smaller or less important trolls and children: well, to everyone really. You can tell she's looking at you and thinking "How *dirty* you children are! And brainless! And noisy! Yuk!"

The **Old Lady** is really a young witch but she does quite a good "sweet old lady" impression. At first she sounds just like your favourite grandmother, though she probably thwacks people with her umbrella more often than your grandmother does. But when she gets angry, her sweet purring voice becomes a snarrrrlll.

The Policeman and **the Teacher** sound bossy. They wouldn't like you, and you definitely wouldn't like them.

The story

A kingdom of Thundertrolls live in the clouds. When they aren't watching Fairy Wrestling on Troll TV, they make lightning bolts and thunder bombs to throw down to earth. Even the littlest Thundertroll makes lightning bolts, which you might already know if you've read the first book of *Wicked Tales*.

The littlest Thundertroll had a dog whose full name was Thoramaguradogg, but everyone called him Trog the Thunderdog. Many years before this story, he was an ordinary dog called Rover. He was owned by a witch who used to tie pretty ribbons onto his collar and use him to catch little children for her supper. But when Rover ate a sausage wand dropped by the Thundertroll Fairy, he was transformed into a Wonder Dog and flew away on a mission to save the world from Bad Cats. That part of his story is told in the first book of *Wicked Tales*. Later on, he got bored with chasing cats: so he became a Thunderdog instead.

Thunderdogs are very important. They chase down stray lightning bolts and bring them back to their masters. Nobody wants a lightning bolt hanging about in their back garden or hiding in the shed… and you really don't want one popping up out of the toilet at the wrong moment.

Catching lightning bolts was hard work, but Trog loved it. Even though he was smaller than the proper Thunderdogs, he was as good at bolt-catching as they were. He did find that his mouth got hot from the fiery bolts, but the other Thunderdogs showed him how to cool off by eating ice from inside the clouds. Nothing makes a Thunderdog happier than a mouthful of crunchy, frozen hailstones.

The Thunder Queen's birthday

One day, there was a big lightning storm party in honour of the Thunder Queen's birthday; hundreds of Thundertrolls gathered in the clouds.

The younger Thundertrolls were standing nervously in a line, with the lightning bolts they'd forged laid out in front of them. They were going to be inspected by the Queen herself, and were very worried about it.

The littlest Thundertroll's mother had spent a long time telling her son what to do.

'You mustn't pick your nose.'

'Or my toes?'

'Not that either.'

'Can I get the fluff out of my belly button?'

'No! Watch what the other trolls do, and copy them.'

'Sooooo…. If they pick their noses, I have to do it too? They do that a lot.'

'No! Maybe it's best if you copy the Queen instead.

Smile like she does and speak politely like she does. If the Queen says hello, you say hello back. If she says she's pleased to meet you, *you* say the same. It's easy!'

'What if she picks the fluff out of her belly button?'

'She won't!'

The Thunder Queen passed down the row of little trolls, patting them on their hard little heads and offering them something from a bag. It was a tradition that Thunder Queens should give out sweets, which they were supposed to make themselves. The Queen didn't like little trolls, so she never bothered to make something nice. This time the Royal Sweets Bag was filled with the first thing she found in her freezer (she was really, really lazy): frozen prawns, which she sprinkled with sugar. She gave a sugar-coated prawn to the littlest Thundertroll and patted him on the head, rather hard.

He thought this was an odd thing for her to do, but he knew he had to copy her: so he patted her – also rather hard - on the leg (that was as high as he could reach).

She thought that was rude, so she gave him a firm tap on his head with a big, poky finger, saying, 'No, no!'

He thought *that* was rude but he had to keep copying, so he tapped her hard on the kneecap with one of his own fingers, also saying, 'No, no!'

She thought that was *very* rude, so she reached down and gave him a firm royal slap on his green troll backside, saying, 'Naughty, naughty!'

And he thought that was *equally* very rude, but he couldn't reach high enough to do the same to her, so as she turned away he took one of his lightning bolts and used that to poke her in… the Royal Backside.

'Naughty, naughty!' he repeated.

'Yiiiiii!' she screamed, dropping most of her prawn sweets. They fell down to earth and bounced about on the ground, scaring a lot of children.

'Uhhh… yiiiii!' he said as well, then threw his own prawn down to the earth… but it slipped out of his hand and hit the Queen on the left big toe instead.

'Yuk!' she cried and threw one of the remaining prawn sweets at the troll. It bounced off his nose and landed in his belly button.

'Dat was very clever!' he said. 'My turn now!'

He threw the prawn back, shouting 'Yuk!' like the Queen. It bounced off *her* nose and landed in *her* belly button. She screamed and grabbed another prawn sweet from the bag and…

… and this might have gone on for a long time if the

Thundertroll King hadn't turned up. He was laughing very loudly at the prawn battle.

'Ho ho, what fun! How are you, little Troll? Still up to your tricks, hey? Ha ha! Do you remember that time when your lightning bolt hit me right in the… ah, right in the *posterior*? And then you climbed onto my head and jumped up and down on it? Hilarious! Ha ha!'

'*Uhhhh… sorry,*' said the littlest Thundertroll.

The King looked at his wife, who still had a prawn in her hand. 'Oh, jolly good!' he boomed. 'Some of your home made sweets, are they? I think I'll try one! You too, little Troll: have one yourself!'

The King took a prawn and put it in his mouth. He gave it a suck. Then he coughed it out, and it landed in the Queen's… belly button.

'That's disgusting!' he shouted.

The littlest Thundertroll put his own prawn in his mouth and coughed it out. '*Disgusting!*' he echoed.

He missed the Queen. But all the other young trolls also put their prawns into their mouths and coughed them out…. And mostly they didn't miss…

The loss of Trog the Thunderdog

The littlest Thundertroll's lightning bolts didn't work very well after that, partly because the Queen had stepped on them while she was hopping about holding her backside. Some bolts shot off towards the pale, distant daytime moon. Some nearly hit his own feet, and one of them burnt off the end of a toenail. Poor Trog the Thunderdog was kept busy chasing the ones that went skittering about the clouds; but he didn't mind. He loved hunting them down!

The final bolt zinged away into the distance, bounced

off a passing airplane and then got trapped in the top of a small, twisty tornado, where it was thrown about by the spinning winds, zooming round and round like an ice cube being stirred in an enormous glass of water by an immense spoon. You would need amazing eyes to see it in the whirling clouds.

Fortunately, Trog the Thunderdog *did* have amazing eyes. He ran to the edge of the spinning tornado and stood there, barking. Every time the lightning bolt came swirling past, he tried to snatch it out; but it was too quick for him and zoomed past before he could get his teeth anywhere near it.

The bolt began to be sucked down into the twister. Trog sat back on his haunches and whined. He didn't like losing one of his master's bolts, but there was nothing he could do about it. Tornados are dangerous: the wind goes round at hundreds of kilometres per hour! He looked down at the disappearing bolt, swirling down and down like a fly being washed down a plug-hole. He looked back at the littlest Thundertroll, who seemed so sad at having lost his last bolt.

Something must be done! And he was Trog, the Good Thunderdog! He must help his master!

So Trog jumped into the tornado.

He went spinning and swirling and spiralling down, down, down until he was totally dizzy. He fell out of the bottom tip of the tornado and rolled over a few times before sitting up and trying to focus his eyes.

He was in the middle of a wide, dusty street. The tornado was disappearing across some fields, taking the lightning bolt with it. He sighed, sat back and scratched one ear. He looked around.

Trog's first good deed

There was a big Bank across the street from Trog. The door to the Bank was flung open suddenly and three men came out. They were carrying heavy bags and had guns in their hands. They looked mean and nasty and very, very pleased with themselves.

Trog didn't like the look of them, so he barked and growled and snarled. The men laughed at him. He started walking forward, growling and baring his big teeth. The men stopped laughing.

They pointed their guns at him. 'Good doggy…nice doggy… go away, nice doggy…'

Trog didn't go away. He got closer. He snarled louder.

They began shooting at him. But he was a Thunderdog who could catch lightning bolts, so catching bullets was easy. He dodged left, right, up, down: and the bullets didn't touch him.

The firing stopped. Trog smiled at the men, his cheeks puffed out with the bullets he'd caught. The men stared at him, then looked at their guns, wondering whether they were loaded with real bullets. One of them shot another bullet. Trog caught it. But he was growling at the same time, so it went down the wrong way – and he coughed – and all the bullets came spraying out like a mouthful of cracker crumbs, but a hundred times as fast and a thousand times as hard.

'Yowwwwwwwww!' cried three gangster voices as their gangster feet were shot full of bullet holes. They fell to the ground and held onto their feet, crying for their Mamas. A few minutes later, the police van came and took them away....

The Witch

Trog trotted away, happy that he had done a Good Deed. He turned off the main road and went down a hill, past a bus stop, past a chocolate shop, past a library, into a park...

He stopped and sat down, puzzling. This place was very familiar. And the figure walking up the road towards him was equally familiar.

The Witch was coming back from her Noggy session. Years ago, as related in the first book of *Wicked Tales*, she had been hit by so many lightning bolts that it made her lose her appetite for eating children. She was very, very upset about this and was having all sorts of treatments to help her get her appetite back. She was trying:

Fakey-Rakey – where people wave tiny rakes over you while making odd humming noises
Reflexy – you get your feet tickled in a special way, which

makes everything better

Hoppy – someone sticks candles in your ears and lights them while frogs dance on your tummy

Yoggy – you sit with eyes closed and knees crossed, chanting funny words while somebody pours yoghurt on your head

Chakrapongy – someone sticks crystals up your nose to re-balance the colour of your aura ("aura" is another name for the gunky stuff under your toenails)

AND IT WORKED! The witch had felt a little better every day, and now – *finally* – she felt like eating little children again... which was bad news for the children... and bad news for Trog.

The witch was walking through the park, looking for her first kiddies takeaway meal for years. Just like in the old days, she had disguised herself as an old lady and was carrying her enormous, super-strong shopping bag, the one she used for catching children.

'Children love ice creams,' she said to herself and took a big frozen ice cream from her bag. She waved it at a little boy walking past.

'Come here, little child!' she called sweetly. 'Granny has a lovely ice cream just for you! And look! There are more of them in my pretty shopping bag. Would you like to look inside it?'

The boy was soaked through from the storm and shivering. He shook his head and ran off. So the witch offered the ice cream to a little girl on a bicycle instead.

'Are you crazy, lady?' the girl asked. 'It's too cold for ice cream!' She laughed and began cycling away slowly, up a steep hill.

The witch snarled and started running after the girl. Then she saw Trog the Thunderdog, and stopped.

Fetching things for a witch

When the witch saw Trog, her eyes lit up and her aura turned a darker shade of purple toenail fluff. 'He's just like Rover!' she exclaimed. 'My little doggy that ran away! Come here, little doggy... I have some lovely doggy nibbles for you... *and then I'll take you home and turn you into a doggy statue for the garden, ha ha!*'

She put down her shopping bag and took a cooked sausage from inside it. She waved it at Trog, who came forward doubtfully, sniffing.

She called sweetly and softly: 'Here, doggy... *here you ugly little dog!* ... See, the sausage is waiting for you... Look in the bag, doggy...' She dropped the sausage into her big bag and held the bag open for Trog. In her free hand she still had the ice cream. Trog looked at the witch. He looked at the bag with the sausage in it.

The old Rover would have put his head in the bag and eaten the sausage. But he was Trog the Thunderdog now! So he jumped high, snatched the ice cream from the witch's hand and began chewing it happily.

'You BAD dog!' the witch exclaimed and reached for her trusty umbrella to thwack him one. But she stopped... smiled... and reached into her bag for Rover's old magic collar. She slipped it around Trog's neck while he was eating the ice cream, and fastened it tight.

'Ha! Now, little doggy: you must do what I say, for this collar puts you in my power! Ha ha!'

Trog finished his ice cream and licked his lips. He wagged his tail, hoping for more icy sweetness. But the witch just laughed at him.

'Go on, little doggy: beg! It won't do you any good, ha ha! No more ice creams for you! That is, unless.... Oh, what a good idea...'

The witch looked up the hill. The little girl was still trying to cycle away, but it was a steep hill and a small girl and a big bike, so it was taking a long time.

'Dinner time!' the witch exclaimed. She took another ice cream from her bag and said to Trog, 'Now, little doggy: would you like this lovely ice cream? Yes? Yes? Then go fetch me that little girl. See her up there? Up *there*, you stupid dog!' She pointed the ice cream to-wards the girl cycling away.

'Fetch!'

Trog jumped up and ate the ice cream.

The witch did pull her umbrella out this time and thwacked him with it, twice. It didn't hurt him much because his head was hard now, like a Thundertroll's.

She pointed at the girl again, with her finger this time: 'Fetch, you stupid dog!'

Trog jumped up and bit … her finger.

'Owwwwww! No, you ugly dog, look at the little child on the bicycle, the one going up the hill!' She took Trog's head between her hands and turned it in the right direction. 'There! Fetch!'

She gave him a good thwack with her umbrella on the backside, launching him up the hill. The little girl saw him coming and screamed. There was a lot of chasing and screaming and shouting and barking and crying. Then the dog came back down the hill…

… riding the bicycle…

... going very fast downhill…

… and then faster …

… and then so fast that his doggy feet couldn't stay on the pedals …

… and then there was an enormous CRASH as he ran the witch down and they both ended up in a ditch.

While they lay there groaning, the little girl came and picked up her bicycle and rode off - down the hill this time - and disappeared from sight.

More fetching

The witch climbed out of the ditch, rubbing her sore bits (which were many) and wiping her muddy bits (which were all over). 'You BAD dog!' she shouted.

Trog whined and hung his head. He didn't want to be a Bad Dog.

She snarled at him, 'It was the child I wanted. *Not* the bike!'

He thumped his tail to show he understood. *No more bicycles*, he said to himself. *She doesn't want a bicycle because they're very hard to ride.*

The witch looked around the park. There were some children playing on the seesaw. Their bicycles were leaning against a nearby tree.

'There! See them, doggy?' She took his head and pointed it at the children. 'See them?'

Trog thumped his tail again.

'Can you fetch me one, doggy? Can you? Can you?'

Trog barked and nodded his head.

'Good dog! Fetch!'

Trog ran off joyfully. *NOT the bicycles*, he reminded himself. *She wants something better to play with. Something that's easier to ride!*

He sped to the seesaw, barking and growling. There was more screaming, crying, howling, followed by biting and catching and dragging.

He was Trog the Thunderdog! He had jaws of steel and could run on the clouds! He returned to the witch, his paws scarcely touching the ground, carrying the whole of the seesaw.

The witch screamed and ran. Trog was pleased. *A game! Catch the witch! Then she'll throw me this big stick to chase!* He ran after her, the seesaw firmly clenched in his jaws. She dodged and jumped, but he was faster. He ran round her and dropped the seesaw at her feet.

Oops. Not at her feet, but *on* her feet.

'Yiiiiiiiowwwww! BAD dog!'

Trog sat down with a sigh. It was going to be hard to make his new master happy…

The Thundertroll's adventure

Meanwhile, the littlest Thundertroll was looking sadly at the empty sky where his beloved dog had been. The tornado had sped away and he didn't know whether Trog was still in the tornado, or on the ground, or had been turned into a million pieces of doggy fluff by the powerful winds.

'I'll find you, Trog!' called the Thundertroll sadly.

'Not today, you won't!' said a stern voice from behind

him. And his mother led him home, saying, 'What were you thinking of? Spitting prawns at the Queen!'

' – She spat them first -'

'And poking her with your light-ning bolts!'

' – She poked me first. And she smacked me on my -'

'Like this?' asked his mother.

'Ouch!'

'You're going straight to your room. And you're going to write a letter to the Queen, apologising for everything!'

'I didn't do *everything*. There's lots of everything and there's only one of me. I haven't got time for *everything*.'

'You'll apologise for all the bad things you did to the Queen!'

'Oh... Will she write me a letter too? For all the bad things *she* did? ...*Ouch!*'

The next morning, the littlest Thundertroll was awake very early. He spent an hour making a very special long-lasting lightning bolt, which he took to the Troll Park in the clouds. He tied one end of it to the lamp post there and then lay on his tummy, peering through the clouds down at the world below.

Where might Trog be? he wondered. The earth was such a big place...

He shook his head sadly. There was no way to know which part of the world Trog had landed in. So... he thought very hard and very slowly, like a rock going for a walk... so... he would go to the only place he knew on the earth: where he'd gone to get a box of chocolates for the Thundertroll Fairy, and had met the witch.

He didn't know she was a witch, of course: he still thought she was just a mean old lady who liked hitting him with her umbrella.

He stood up, took his lightning bolt in his hand, aimed carefully and threw it as hard as he could. Then he jumped off the cloud and rode the bolt down to earth.

ZING ZONG ZANG THWWWWWANG!

It hit the top of a lamp post in the middle of a park down below: a park where everything looked exactly as it should, except that the seesaw was missing.

He tied the lightning bolt to the top of the lamp post in the Earth Park and slid down the post. He began walking downhill, towards the main road.

The policeman

A policeman came in through the park gates at the bottom, swinging his truncheon. When he saw the Thundertroll, he stopped and stared.

This is not surprising: you would probably stare, too. The Thundertroll was short and square and green… and didn't wear any clothes.

'Hey, you! Boy! Come here! *Now!*' commanded the policeman.

The Thundertroll walked up to him, smiling.

'What are you doing here, funny looking boy?'

'I'm looking for my dog, funny looking man. Have you seen a little dog?'

The policeman said bossily, 'Have you seen a little dog, *please?*'

The Thundertroll replied, 'No... I haven't. That's why I'm asking you!'

The policeman looked at him sternly. 'What's your name, boy?' he asked. 'And your answer had better be respectful!'

The Thundertroll said, 'Respectful? Mummy never called me Respectful, so dat can't be my name.'

'What's – your - name?!'

'No, dat isn't my name either. She never called me Whats. You want to guess again? Dis is a good game!'

The policeman said slowly, 'I want you to tell me your name, and I want you to do it now, and I want you to say Please and Thank you and call me Sir!'

'Oh.... Is dat your name?'

The policeman repeated slowly: 'Is - that - your – name - *please* - sir?'

'No, Sir isn't my name. I thought it was yours!'

The policeman shook his truncheon at the Thundertroll. 'That's *not* my name!' he shouted.

'Oh... Is it your dog's name?'

'I haven't got a dog!'

'Why not?'

'Because – because I don't!'

'Who catches your lightning bolts for you, then?'

'What?! That's enough of your questions! You'll have to answer *mine* now! And say please!'

'Please.'

The policeman took a deep breath before asking, 'Why aren't you at school?'

The Thundertroll put his head to one side and thought about this for a long time. Then he said, 'I give up. What's the answer?'

'You silly boy! Do you want to get into trouble?'

'Uh... I don't think so... What's it like?'

The Thundertroll smiled at the policeman, who was jumping up and down with rage. Then he asked the policeman, 'Why aren't *you* at school?'

'I don't go to school!' the man shouted. 'And you have to say please!'

'Oh... Do *you* have to say please, too? Or is it something you only have to say if you're looking for your dog? Uhhh...please.'

'I'm a grown up,' said the policeman. 'I don't have to say please to children!'

'Even when you're looking for your dog? Please.'

The policeman took another deep breath. 'Look, boy: you ought to be in school. I know which school you go to, because you're wearing a green uniform. The only school in this town that wears green is St Patrick's Primary. So I'm going to take you there. Now.'

The troll shook his head. He said, 'Dis isn't my clothes. Dis is my skin! ...Please.'

The policeman stared at him. 'It can't be. Nobody has green skin! That's your school uniform. But how do you put it on? You don't have any zips or buttons!'

'I got one button – look – it's my belly button! Please!'

'Stop saying please all the time!'

'Oh. All right.... Please.'

The policeman led him to the school and delivered him to the classroom door of 3B. The Thundertroll waved goodbye to him happily.

'Goodbye Mister Sir! I liked our game! Please!'

'Don't say please!'

'I won't! Please!'

Thundertroll at school

The teacher's name was Miss Bossy. She looked at the

littlest Thundertroll, then pointed at a chair in the far corner of the room.

He went and picked up the chair and brought it to Miss Bossy.

'No!' she said. 'I want you to sit on it!'

He put the chair down and sat on it.

'No! Back over there, where the chair was!'

The Thundertroll said, 'Oh. Sorry... Please!' He took the chair back and sat on it again, at a little table.

She came to his table, holding a sheet of paper and a pencil. 'I want you to write your name on this paper, please,' she said briskly.

'Dat isn't my name. Please.'

'What isn't your name?'

'*Please* isn't my name. Uh... please.'

'Stop saying please!'

'But Miss, you said it first! Please!'

He reached for the pencil she was holding out, but she pulled it back and wagged a finger at him.

She said, 'Look here, smelly green child: when I offer you a pencil, what do you say?'

She held out the pencil again. He looked at it.

'I say... Hello pencil! Please!'

'No! You say *thank you*. *Please* when you want something, *thank you* when you get it.'

'But I didn't want a pencil....'

'That doesn't matter! You should always say thank you! Say it!' She offered him the paper this time.

'Uh...Hello paper! Please and thank you!'

'That's better. Now write your name on the paper.'

'Uh... Mummy never gave me one.'

'What does she call you?'

'Sweetie Pie. But mostly she calls me You Bad Boy.'

'That's your name, then: YouBadBoy. Write it down. Then draw me a picture of your mother.'

She left him. He puzzled for a while, then drew a lightning bolt on one side of the paper: that would do for his name. He turned it over and began drawing carefully. When the teacher returned, she screamed.

'What on earth is that?' she exclaimed.

'Mummy!' he said.

'But it looks like the inside of a big nose!'

'Yeah dat's right. Dat's what I see when I look up at a grown up. The paper was too small to put all of her on, so I drew the only bit of her small enough to fit!'

The teacher put a big red X on the drawing. 'Try again!' she said. 'Go get some more paper from the box! Use a larger piece if you want to draw a bigger picture!' She pointed to the front of the classroom.

The Thundertroll walked to the cardboard box. There were many sizes of paper in it, but he shook his head at them all.

'Miss! I need something bigger! Please and thank you!'

'Then *find* something bigger! I'm busy!'

The Thundertroll looked all around. He picked up a large crayon. When the teacher next turned around, she screamed again.

'What's that?' she cried out, pointing at an enormous, scary drawing on the classroom wall.

'Mummy!' the Thundertroll answered. 'I got most of her on it this time! Thank you! And please!'

Sharing

Soon it was lunchtime. The littlest Thundertroll didn't have anything to eat but he didn't mind. He could still taste the prawn sweets the Queen had given them, and all he wanted was a long drink of water to rinse the taste away. So he went to the pond and had a good, long slurp. A dinner lady caught him and told him off.

He went to play with the other children, but they ran away because he was large and green and naked; and he had pond weed on his head, with pond creatures dancing about in it. The same dinner lady came to see what was going on, and told him off for not having proper buttons on his shirt. So he drew some buttons on his front with a crayon.

He joined in a game of catch but he didn't understand that you had to give the ball back. All the children chased him up and down the playground until the dinner lady caught him and told him he had to SHARE.

'Why?' he asked.

'You just do,' she said, taking the ball from him and throwing it to the other children.

'Oh.... Does everybody have to share? Or only if they have a green tummy button?'

'*Everybody* should share.'

'Hooray!' he said. 'Can I have your shoes? I like dem!'

'No!'

'Oh... Can I have your buttons, den? Dat would be better than drawing 'em on my chest!'

'No!'

'Oh... Don't we share buttons?'

'We only share things like toys - and food – and – and -'

'Chickens?'

'No!'

'Mummies?'

'No!!!'

'Can I have some food, den? You said we share food.'

'Didn't you have any lunch?'

He said sadly, 'Mummy never gave me none.'

'You poor child. I think we have some pizza left in the kitchen.'

She led him to the kitchen, where there was an enormous pizza in a tin, going cold.

'Hooray!' he shouted. 'I like sharing!' And he swallowed the pizza whole.

More sharing

The next lesson was his favourite because they were given lots of paper and glue and sticks and scissors and told to make things.

He made something very scary, and several children began to cry.

'What's that statue supposed to be?' asked the teacher. 'It's horrible!'

'Dat's the Thunder Queen!' he said.

'What's that funny square green thing she's kicking?'

'Dat's me!'

'And what does she have in her hand?'

'Prawn sweets!'

'That's the worst statue I've ever seen!'

'Thank you! Uhhh...Please and thank you!'

The teacher looked at what the boy next to him had been making. 'That's lovely, Billy,' she said. 'Is that a fluffy white cloud you've made out of cotton wool?'

'Yes, Miss. And it's got a big thunderbolt coming out of it. See? Zap!'

'Good boy, Billy.' She patted him on the head.

She turned to the Thundertroll and said, 'Look what a nice picture Billy's made. *And* he made a big thunderbolt using some shiny foil! Why don't you make a thunderbolt, YouBadBoy?'

The Thundertroll grinned. 'I can make a real thunderbolt!' he said.

'No you can't.'

'Uhhhh... I can! Thank you!'

'Don't be silly. Look, here's some shiny foil and some scissors. Make a thunderbolt with them. Like Billy's.'

'A real one? Please and thank you?'

She sighed. 'All right,' she said. 'Make a *real* thunderbolt. Then we can share it with the other children during Assembly.'

'Hooray! I like sharing! You get pizza when you share!'

At the end of school, all the children came together in Assembly. It was the turn of Miss Bossy's class to show what they had been doing, so some of her children were called to the front, where they held up lumps of clay that looked like badly designed animals, or waved pictures that looked like nothing on earth.

Then Miss Bossy announced, 'Our newest student has made us something special: he says it's a *real* lightning bolt! YouBadBoy, come and show the rest of the school!'

The littlest Thundertroll walked to the front, grinning all over. He had all his schoolwork in his arms.

'I got dis picture of Mummy's nose...' (screams from the children) '... and dis statue of the Queen...' (more screams and howls of terror) '...and dis lightning bolt!'

He waved something thin and jagged and very bright.

One little girl said scornfully, 'It's a very *small* lightning bolt!'

A big boy laughed at it. 'It isn't real! *Na na na na na!*'

Miss Bossy said, 'Of course it isn't real. But it's very clever and I think we ought to give YouBadBoy a round of applause.'

'I don't want a round of apples,' said the littlest Thun-dertroll. 'I just had pizza.'

'Throw the lightning bolt!' shouted some big kids at the back.

'No. Someone might get hurt,' said the Thundertroll.

'Throw it! Throw it!' all the children chanted.

'I think you'll have to throw it,' whispered Miss Bossy. 'Just throw it down in front of the little ones. You have to share, you know!'

'All right,' said the Thundertroll...

ZAP!

The witch looks for her dinner

Meanwhile, the witch had put on her very best Old Lady disguise. She picked up her umbrella and her super-size shopping bag, then called:

'Walkies! Come with Granny, little doggy!'

Trog the Thunderdog trotted up and let her attach the dog lead to his magic collar. She opened the door and stepped out.

'Heel!' she ordered.

So Trog bit her on the heel.

'Yowwww! Bad dog! Take that!'

Thwack thwack thwack went the umbrella.

'Take *that* -'

Trog took the umbrella.

The witch grabbed it and pulled, shouting, 'No! Let go of it! Let go!'

Trog let go, and she fell into her own shopping bag.

Her backside was bigger than the rest of her, so she was stuck there for several minutes, with her legs and arms poking out the top. When the bag fell over, she finally managed to squeeze out.

She stood up and pointed her umbrella at Trog. 'Bad dog! *Very* bad dog!'

Trog whined and hung his head again. He was trying his best.

They walked to the park together, with the witch explaining her plan to Trog. 'Lots of lovely little children go through the park on their way home,' she said. 'Sometimes a very tasty one comes through all alone, and then – GOTCHA! – into the shopping bag he goes!'

Rachel

Trog barked and wagged his tail. He didn't understand what the witch was going on about, but he liked playing *Gotcha* with lightning bolts, so this was going to be fun.

The first children – big ones - came past in a big group, laughing. The witch waited.

Then a lot of little ones ran past, crying and howling. Some of them smelled of burning.

Then Miss Bossy stamped past, carrying her briefcase. She looked very angry.

A motorcycle came wobbling through the park gates, with something green and lumpy on it. The Thundertroll shouted, 'Thanks for sharing your funny wheely thing, Miss Bossy! It's fun! Please and thank you!'

Miss Bossy turned around and ran down the hill. She knocked the Thundertroll off the motorcycle with her briefcase. Then she jumped on the motorbike, gunned the throttle and zoomed away, wheels screeching and motor racing.

The littlest Thundertroll got up from the ditch he had fallen into and began walking up the hill. The witch peered at him. He looked familiar... but he also looked plump and juicy and very, very tasty. She pointed at him with a long, bony finger.

'Fetch!' she commanded Trog. 'Owwww! *Not* my finger again! Fetch the *little boy*! See him? Go get him! Go! Good dog!'

Trog quivered all over with joy. He *was* a good dog! And – and there was his master, walking up the hill towards him with his arms wide! Trog leapt down the hill and landed on the Thundertroll's chest; they rolled over and over, barking and talking happily.

The witch came up. 'Good dog!' she said to Trog. 'You got him!'

She dropped the bag over the Thundertroll's head and pulled it down over his shoulders. She led him away, cackling to herself.

'Dis is a good game!' said the littlest Thundertroll. 'We can play dis back home, Trog!' But since his head and half his body were covered by a large bag, that sentence came out as DsDdDame...EcdPayDisHomeTog!

Ready... steady... cook!

When they got to the witch's house, she locked the doors before taking the bag off the Thundertroll's head.

'You wait here, little boy,' she cooed. 'I'll make us some lovely dinner. Ha ha!'

She went and found her largest roasting pan. 'Now, little boy: sit in this special car. Oooh – it's just the right size for you, ha ha! Look, you can ride in it. I'll pull you into the kitchen on it, shall I? Oh... ouch... you're *very* heavy; I'll get the dog to help. Come doggy! Push!'

'Dis is fun!' shouted the Thundertroll as they dragged him through the house and up to the hot oven, which she opened. It was an ENORMOUS oven – big enough to put a little child in.

The witch cried out, 'Ooooo look, little boy! The car has turned into a magic flying carpet! It can fly into this big warm cave!'

However, the Thundertroll was too heavy for her to lift. 'Help me lift, doggy!' she called. 'Put him in the oven! I mean, in the *big warm cave*!'

The Thundertroll got out of the pan, put the dog in the pan, and lifted it into the oven.

No!' screamed the witch. 'Take the dog out!'

The Thundertroll was puzzled. 'You said, Help me lift doggy. Put him in the oven. So I did.'

'No! I was talking to the doggy, not to you! Get back in the roasting pan – I mean in the *magic flying carpet*. Doggy, see if you can put the little boy inside the warm cave by yourself this time.'

Trog was very strong. He picked up the tray and put the Thundertroll in... the tumble drier.

'No! Look, little doggy. Here's a cake I made this morning. Watch me put it in the oven – in the *warm cave*. Put the little boy in the nice warm cave like *this*.'

She lifted the cake from the table and put it in the oven, then took it out again. 'See how easy it is? Your turn, doggy!'

Trog picked up the cake and put in the oven.

'No!!!'

Trog took the cake out of the oven and put it in the washing machine.

'No!!! You stupid dog! *Bad* dog!'

by Marta

Trog wagged his tail sadly.

Trog by David

'Not the cake! The little boy!'

Trog brightened. He took the cake from the washing machine and gave it to the Thundertroll, who ate it in one big gulp. 'Dat was good! Please and thank you!'

'No! Doggy, put the boy *in*!'

Trog put the Thundertroll in the washing machine, where the cake had been.

'No!!!! Take him out!'

Trog took the Thundertroll out of the washing machine and tried to put him in the breadbin.

'Oh, you nitwits! You noodles! You ninny numskull nerdy noggin nimby-nambies! Do I have to show you again? Look!'

The witch pointed at the Thundertroll.

'Boy!' she snarled. Then she pointed to the oven.

'Oven!' she shouted. 'I mean - *warm cave!*'

Then she screeched, '*In!* Like this!'

She climbed into the oven. '*In!*' she called back to them, her muffled voice echoing.

A few moments later, she called, 'Help me OUT!' But all they heard was '*OUT!*'. So they went *out* into the garden, closing the kitchen door behind them.

Endings

The tornado had come back. It was wandering along the road quite slowly, like a boy looking for pennies in the gutter. Something shiny was whizzing about near its base.

'Look, Trog – dere's my lightning bolt! Fetch!'

Joyfully, Trog the Thunderdog ran to the tornado and then ran around and round it, trying to catch up with the spinning bolt. Finally he dived into the whirling winds and emerged from the other side, the bolt clenched in his jaws.

'Good dog!' cried the Thundertroll, running up and patting him on the head.

Trog thumped his tail happily. He *was* a good dog! Hooray!

They made their way back to the park, where they climbed the lamp post and found the long lightning bolt tied to its top. They rode it back up to the clouds, talking and barking happily.

… Meanwhile, a muffled voice was heard in a certain kitchen.

'Is anybody there? Hello?'

There was a sound of rushing wind outside.

'Little boy? Little doggy? My big backside is stuck in this oven – this big warm cave. Well, it's quite a *hot* cave now…. Could you -'

The wind whistled and swirled about the house. The house began to rise.

'Hello?'

The house disappeared into the tornado, together with the hot oven and the hot witch… and I hope that was the very last thing she cooked.

Georgina and the Dragon

The voices

The Witch sounds smooth and calm and totally in control, loving every moment of her sneakiness. Disposing of princes? Cheating her own clients? Lying to everyone? She *loves* it. The only time she loses her cool is when Georgina stands up to her.

Princess Georgina sounds clever and confident, as if being locked in a high tower is quite amusing, really. You can tell she's as tough as the stones in the tower. She's more than a match for the witch and her devious uncle.

Baron Cheatalot has a large, round voice to go with his large, round body. He sounds pleased with himself: and so he should be. He's had a lazy, selfish life full of food and wine and more food. He hasn't had to work except on Tuesdays. And he's just about to get all the Princess's money, as well as the Kingdom.

Fearsome the Dragon talks a bit like your best friend. He's kind and funny; and he gets really excited about games and adventures and playing Dragonchase in the sky after dark. He's not worried about being useless at scaring princes and gobbling princesses. The only thing that really bothers him is the way his parents keep nagging him to be like the other dragons.

Fearsome's parents sound like most parents: worried about their children... wanting the best for them... not really understanding how their children feel... expecting their children to eat everything on their plates, even the green bits and the curried Royals.

The Princes sound spoiled: they're soooo smooth, confident and full of their own importance; but ignorant of things that matter, such as the fact that the Royal Coaster Ride has no brakes.

The story

The scary amusement park

Once upon a time there was a very clever witch who ran what looked like an amusement park. In reality, it was a front for her two other businesses – the Royalty Disposal Service and Royalty R We.

The three businesses worked hand in hand. Let's say you're King Grunthog and you want to get rid of your two annoying cousins, Prince Slob and Princess Slobberina. Simple! You phone the Royalty Disposal Service, tell them your credit card number and – lo and behold, with a flourish of trumpets! – the two brats receive a special invitation to the Royalty Amusement Park. They play on the Bouncy Castle, scream on the Royal Coaster and then disappear somewhere between the Death Slide and the Big Chopper.

While the two Royal Rejects are being chained down in the Dungeon of Doom, another phone call might be received - by Royalty R We this time. The lady on the other end is looking for a gardener or cleaner of royal blood; more money changes hands; then dear Slob and Slobberina find themselves working as servants in the darkest parts of Outer Slum-pong, or even Basingstoke.

Although royals are seldom any good at cleaning, gardening, cooking, washing, writing books or even brushing their teeth, they are *very* decorative; and it makes a big impression on guests when a dippy looking girl wearing a crown passes around the party nibbles.

For the royals who arrived for Royal Disposal, there were some wonderful activities, such as:

* Save the Princess from the Dragon! (with a real dragon but a plastic, blow-up princess)
* Bungee Jump in Legless Land without a Rope!
* Deep Sea Driving through the Monster Moat!
* Shop till you Drop! (you wander around a store trying to find a royal duvet & pillow set, until you accidentally get onto the Endless Escalator of Doom).

Photos were taken of princes doing manly things and princesses doing fluffy things; these were displayed on the Royalty R We site, so that people shopping for royals could choose the one they liked.

Sadly, like the ugly kitten or puppy at the animal shelter, there were some princes that no one wanted, and even a few princesses gazing sadly from the Bargain

Basement page, or (even worse) the Dungeon Deal page. I can't bear to tell you what happened to these…

Not all the princes at the park were there for disposal. Many royals and wannabe royals came just for the fun; and if they didn't make it back home, nobody usually noticed. In fact, the witch needed all these extra princes turning up and tried hard to attract more. She spent a lot of time on the phone to Queens and Kings, encouraging them to send their little darlings out to play and answering their questions, such as:

'I say – this Bungee jumping without a rope thingy… Isn't that a little dangerous?'

'Yes, a *little*. But we're fully insured.'

'That's all right then! I'll send all twelve of our boys!'

Baron Cheatalot

Sadly, the amusement park was having a hard time. The Bouncy Castle was going flabby. The Monster Moat had sprung a leak. And although the dragon was real enough, the princess was clearly fake. This was a big problem, because word was getting out that once you'd got past the bad breath and sharp teeth, your only reward was a kiss from an inflatable doll.

That's why the witch was soooooo excited when she got a phone call from Baron Cheatalot. He said:

'Sadly, my brother the King died in an unfortunate accident involving a bathtub, a lawnmower and an electric chainsaw. Then his wife the Queen tripped while mowing the moat. So I'm the King now: Hooray! Except - of course – I'm really just looking after the throne for little Georgina until she reaches 21 later this year. And dear, sweet Georgina is a Problem Child. Unlike her parents, she isn't accident prone at all, however hard we try.… So I was wondering: could we send her to visit your lovely Amusement Park? And if she likes it so much that she doesn't come back, then – well - we would understand, you know.'

The witch said, 'Many royal visitors take up the Extended Stay option. However, princesses are *very* expensive to look after. The dresses, the shoes, the make up, the shoes, the handbags, the ponies. Not to mention the shoes.' As she said this, she put her feet on the desk and studied her black leather ballet pumps studded with real diamonds, pearls and sharks' teeth.

'Of course!' said the Baron. 'I realise we will have to pass over a small amount of gold if she stays at the park. Fortunately, the old King and Queen left behind a pile of treasure for the Princess. I'm looking after it for the dear child: Hooray!'

by Marta

The witch asked, 'Is the Princess pretty?'

'Only at a distance.'

'Stupid?'

'Sadly, no. She beats everyone at chess and jigsaws and even Snap.'

'What a shame,' said the witch. 'I do need a princess at the park: to attract the princes you know. But they prefer cute girls who don't know their times tables.'

'How right you are! She's far too clever to be a Royal. The only thing in her favour is her lovely long hair, like the princess in that old story. It's as long as a – as a –'

'As long as a tower is high?'

'Yes! As long as that!'

'Ha ha!' exclaimed the witch. 'Perfect! I know just the thing for her!'

The Princess is imprisoned

And so the fate of Princess Georgina was sealed. She duly arrived on a Saturday, attended by three maids who carried most of her hair behind her and a fourth pushing a wheelbarrow which held the rest of it. And it was true: she was as ordinary-looking as you or me, but her hair was long and beautiful.

by Simona

She had difficulty doing some of the activities, but she looked perfectly lovely on the Royal Coaster with her hair streaming out behind her like a great flying snake until it got tangled in the wheels of the fifteenth car behind her, causing the car to leave the tracks and Prince Numskull to leave this world an hour before he was planned to. She won lots of prizes on the Peasant Shooting stall - and the Guess the Wait at the Royal Call Centre - and the Boring Celebrity Trivia slot machines. Then she was fed ice creams and cotton candy and sugared almonds and popcorn and milk shakes until she was ready to burst.

Lastly, she was shown the Tower of Tribulation. She was standing in the paved plaza at its base, looking up at the tiny window far, far above her when an attractive lady dressed in black and silver glided across the pavement and touched her on the arm.

This lady was the witch, but you wouldn't have guessed it unless you knew that witches always wear their hair a certain way and usually dress in something very expensive (*Because we're worth it!* they say).

'Would you like to climb to the top, my dear?' asked the witch, bowing and curtseying and pretending to be ever so nice and sweet and very, very rich.

The Princess looked at her closely before answering. 'No thank you, scary old lady. I'm full of junk food and I might spew it up all over the handsome princes wandering around down here.'

The witch snorted angrily, 'Old? *I'm* not old! Look: I'm wearing high heeled shoes with gold trimmings and a teensy-tiny skirt and have a fashionable handbag! I'm very young and very rich and I own this lovely park. Would you like me to order my servants to carry you up the three hundred steps, dear Princess?'

The Princess replied, 'No thank you, old lady pretending to be a young one, with too many shoes and an evil glint in her eye. You can't trick me into going up there.'

The witch said angrily, 'Oh, so you think you're *clever*, do you? You're not as clever as you think you are!'

Princess Georgina answered, 'No, but I'm much cleverer than you think I think I am, not to mention being cleverer than you think you know you are. And by the way, your handbag is last year's fashion and those overpriced shoes ought to be sold so you can help poor children with the money.'

The witch turned pink, stamped one expensive foot and clapped her hands. 'Park Helpers!' she called. 'All Helpers to me!'

About a hundred Helpers came running, most of them dressed as cute animals. She pointed to some of the bigger ones.

'Bears 1 to 4! Pigs 1 to 8! Reindeers 5 and 6! The Princess wants to be carried up the tower. Take her *now*! And Donkeys 4 to 9 – get rid of those ladies in waiting!'

'But -' Georgina began; but it was too late. While the donkeys chased away the Princess's attendants, the bears lifted her and turned her onto her side. The reindeers used their antlers to spin her around and around (rather like a chicken being turned on a barbecue spit) and the pigs pushed her hair about so that as she spun, she was wrapped up inside a huge spool of her own hair, like a great ball of garden twine.

Then the bears carried the hairy, wriggling bundle up the three hundred steps to the very top of the tower. They put her on a spinning platform with a pole poking out of the middle, rather like the ones you find in a playground. The witch grabbed the end of her hair, gave it a pull and flung it out the window. The Princess unwound like a spinning top and her lovely hair cascaded to the ground (well, almost to the ground – it was about a metre short).

When poor Georgina had stopped spinning and was able to see straight again, she found she was in a tiny room with a chair, a table, a spinning playground ride and a witch wearing an evil smirk and ruby slippers (she had changed shoes before climbing the stairs).

'Ha ha! Who's the clever one now?' the witch boasted.

'I've caught you and you're *mine*! You can't get away! Ha ha!'

'Yes I can,' said the Princess. 'Any time I like, in fact.'

'Oh yes? Do it, then!'

'I'll do it when I want to.'

'You're lying!'

'I never lie. It's a *bad* thing to do.'

The witch grabbed the Princess by the shoulder and dragged her over to the window. 'Look down there!' she gloated. 'Look at all those princes so far below that they look like ants!'

'No,' said the Princess. 'They look like small princes. Ants are a completely different shape and have six legs. But you're right about one thing: it is a long way down and it makes me feel very dizzy looking at it.'

'Ha ha! So you agree: you *are* trapped up here! The door to this room will be locked; and if you jumped out the window, my pretty, you'd go down, down, down, *splat*! Ha ha! Hee hee!'

'I'm not pretty and I'm not yours and I won't go *splat*. But you'd better stop making me look down there. I don't enjoy it.'

'Ha ha! Now you've said that, I'll make you look for even longer!'

'You'll regret it. And so will the princes.'

'No we won't!'

The Princess was suddenly very, very sick out the window.

by Marta

'I think *they* regret it,' she said, pointing at the screaming princes below.

The new ride at the park

The Rapunzel Ride was a great success. Hundreds of princes came to the park just to try it, and mostly the Ride went like this:

'Rapunzel, Rapunzel, let down your golden hair, that I might climb your golden stair!'

'Why?'

'Because… oh gosh… I don't really know why, but I think I need to climb up there in order to save you.'

'I don't want to be saved.'

'Oh, but surely the ogre – or giant - or evil wizard thingy up there needs to be conquered. And I, the strong and handsome but rather dim prince have come to do just that. I will save you, Rapunzel, you sad, weak, pathetic maiden. Rapunzel, Rapunzel, let down –'

'I'm not sad, I'm not weak, I'm not pathetic and that's **not** my name!'

'Oh…. It isn't? Just a moment.' (Looks at leaflet in hand). 'No, I've got the right name. You *are* Rapunzel, it says so here in black and silver. Look, sweetie: just let your long, gorgeous hair down, would you? People are laughing at me down here.'

'If you insist. But you'll be sorry!'

The lovely hair would fall, the prince would grab it, then begin the long climb upwards while "Rapunzel" sat and read a book. She had already wound her hair around the post a few times so that the prince's weight couldn't pull her out the window and didn't yank bits of her hair from her scalp: that really hurt.

Up the prince would climb, and further up, and – well, sometimes he fell off and landed on a little trampoline (or missed it, if the witch had ordered it to be removed as he climbed); or else he reached the top, when he would pose at the window for his friends to take pictures of him in all his manly power and glory before climbing inside, never to be seen again.

The Princess quickly got bored with manly princes leaping through the window, demanding a kiss and then being dragged away by Bears 3 to 7 or Lions 1 to 4.

From time to time the witch would climb the steps in her latest expensive shoes, cackle with delight and say something like, 'I see you haven't worked out how to get away yet, Clever Clogs!'

The Princess replied, 'There's nothing clever about clogs and I can get away any time I like.'

'How?'

'You'll find out. But only when it's too late!'

Fearsome the Dragon

Meanwhile, the Dragon in the Park was very unhappy. He'd only taken this job because his mother had nagged him every day to do something with his life.

'You can't stay in the cave with us forever, you know!' she'd say.

'Why not?'

'Because, Fearsome dear, you're all grown now up and you need your own cave. And a dragon wife. *And a job!*

'Why?'

'You just do. You're ten years old now! When your father was ten, he'd already burned down seven barns.'

'Don't like burning things.'

'And he'd eaten twenty maidens!'

'Don't like the taste of humans.'

'You don't like *anything*!'

'I like playing games. I'm good at games.'

'Well, you're not staying home all day playing on your D-Box. Off you go to the Job Centre and find a proper job, like scaring sheep.'

'I've tried that. I can't scare anything. I'm *not* scary! Everybody says so.'

Fearsome the Dragon had always been teased and mocked and laughed at by the other dragons at school. He was called rude names like *Nice* and *Kind* and *Friendly* and *Couldn't Scare a Kitten*. He was good at active games like Dragonball and clever games like Dragonopoly, but he could never learn the things his teachers tried to explain in class: how to chase children, how to swallow a sheep without getting the wool stuck in your teeth, how to peel the armour off a knight. He had even failed his SATS – the Scary Attainment Tests.

His mother looked at him fondly. 'I'm sure you could be scary if you really tried, dear,' she said. 'And I've seen a perfect job for you advertised on the DragonNet: one where you could practise being... well, fearsome.'

So he'd ended up at the Royalty Adventure Park, pretending to be a savage dragon who was just about to eat a frightened princess. The pay was good and he could have as many burgers and chips as he liked, so long as he flew in with a tree for firewood every morning and lit the Park fires before he started work.

But it was embarrassing to be up here on the top of Dragon Mountain with a large blow-up rubber doll; still more embarrassing when the latest prince climbed up with a princely swagger, pulled out his sword, then laughed and said, 'Hey, dragon – that *doll* is scarier than *you* are!'

The dragon had orders not to eat the princes (not that he wanted to) but he always gave them a light toasting before the bears, lions or wolves took them away.

This went on week after week, and he *hated* it. But – as his mother often told him - it's important to do a job well even if you don't enjoy it much. So he did his best to scare the princes. He roared, breathed fire, filled the air with smoke, then sliced the smoke into ribbons with his long, curved claws. But after a few seconds of horror, the prince's face would break into a smile and he would call out something like, 'What-ho! *This* is a jolly game, isn't it? I say, you wouldn't happen to know where I can get a cup of tea up here, would you?'

The wonderful meeting

One day Fearsome arrived at work as usual, but as he flew in with his load of firewood he saw something he hadn't noticed before: a maiden standing at the window of the tower, her long golden hair flashing in the morning sunlight.

His mountain was behind the tower, so normally he didn't see the front. He had been wondering why so many princes were visiting there; now he knew. He was a curious dragon, so after he'd dropped off his firewood, he went to investigate.

He flew to the big window and hovered there, flapping his wings slowly, looking at the beautiful princess. Beautiful to *him*, that is: the princes were always disappointed when they got to the top and saw her up close.

Fearsome the Dragon didn't know what to say, so he said the first thing that popped into his head:

'Want a few games of Snapdragon?'

'Why – why - I'd love it!' exclaimed the startled Princess. 'But I warn you, I'm very good at games. By they way, I'm Georgina, *aka* Rapunzel'.

'I'm Fearsome, *aka* Not Fearsome at All.'

So Fearsome flew up to the window and pulled out his Snapdragon cards (he always carried some with him). He won the first three games easily. Then the Princess won three; and they were having a mighty tussle in the deciding game when there was a shout from below:

'Rapunzel, Rapunzel -'

'What NOW?' the Princess shouted down. She leaned out over the window ledge and shook her fist at the tiny figure below. 'Can't you princes leave me alone for a moment?'

The prince below shouted back, 'Could you hurry up and throw your hair down, sweetie? I've got an appointment to have my nails polished at noon! Come on, my lovely: give it to me!'

'Give it to you? Right then - catch!' the Princess shouted, emptying a bucket out the window.

A certain amount of screaming followed. The dragon looked puzzled.

'Chamber pot,' explained the Princess. 'They don't have toilets up here.'

'That was a bit mean,' said the dragon. 'You've got to make allowances for princes, you know. They aren't as bright as their subjects.'

'That shouldn't stop them being polite!' snapped the Princess. Then she snapped again, putting down a card: 'SNAP!'

'DRAGON!' the dragon shouted back. 'I won!'

Princess Georgina looked at the cards he'd laid on the table. 'So you did! That's amazing! I've never lost a Snapdragon match before!'

'Shall we try something new? Parcheesi?

'Salami?' she shot back, because she liked playing with words too.

'Macaroni!'

An Alice dragon

'Trigonometry!'

'Hyperchondria!'

'Hemidemisemiquavers!'

The both laughed until the tears ran down their faces (rather steamy, sizzling tears for the dragon).

They settled to a game of Chess, which the Princess won easily, then one of Mancala which the dragon won, then Racing Demon which was a very exciting tie.

'I've got to go to work now,' sighed the dragon (setting light to the playing cards as he did so).

'Me too,' said the Princess. 'Same tomorrow?'

'Snap!' said the Dragon.

'Crackle!'

'Poppadums!'

'See you tomorrow, Dragon.'

'See you, Princess.'

They met every morning that month, and sometimes in the evenings too. When they ran out of games, they invented new ones. The dragon brought a tower-building game called Tonga. When the tower had fallen over twice in the usual way, they played Blind Tonga (you close your eyes before taking out a piece part way up and place it on top), then Back-handed Tonga (you use the wrong hand), then Back-handed Blind Tonga, then Upside-down Back-handed Blind Tonga (you start with a tower built with gaps, close your eyes, take a piece from the top with your wrong hand, then push it into one of the holes).

'Tonga!' Fearsome shouted as the tower fell.

'No, that's *wronga*!' said the Princess. 'You should have shouted *Agnot* because it was back-handed!'

'*Vguof* since it's upside down and backward.'

'We can do a *Nagto* version if we start in the middle.'

'Ognat!'

'GoAnt!'

It all goes wrong

After a month, the dragon plucked up courage to tell his parents over breakfast one morning.

'I've been seeing this princess at the Park, right?'

'Yummy!' shouted his father.

'Did you roast her first or steam her lightly? Or steep her in smoke?' asked his mother.

'No,' said Fearsome. 'We just talk and play games.'

'Oh. You mean, chasing games?' asked his father.

'And biting off little bits of her?' asked his mother.

'And making her scream a lot, I hope?'

'And squeal? That's very important, the squealing. Sign of a professional job when they scream *and* squeal.'

'*And* faint with terror, son. I hope you're giving her time to faint once or twice before you eat her!'

Fearsome roared at his parents, 'I knew you wouldn't understand!'

'Understand what, my boy?' asked his mother.

Fearsome said, 'We play fun games. No screaming. Just a lot of laughter.'

His parents stared at him. His mother's lower lip quivered.

Dragon by Ben

Fearsome explained, 'I like her. She likes me. We're - we're friends.'

They stared some more, aghast. Then his father rumbled, 'That's not normal.'

His mother began to weep. 'I always knew,' she said. 'I always told your father - didn't I, dear? - that there was something wrong with our little boy. He didn't play biting games, didn't chase sheep after school with the other boys, didn't eat his curried Royals...'

Fearsome said, 'There's nothing wrong with me. For the first time ever, I feel right.'

His father said, 'But humans are our enemies! They hunt us, we burn them to smithereens! Or eat them.'

'It doesn't have to be like that, Dad.'

'What will the neighbours say?' wailed his mother. She pointed at Fearsome's father. 'This comes from your side of the family!' she accused. 'Your Uncle Smokey went vegetarian! And Great Grandpa Firestorm used to sneak into Churches and knew all the hymns by heart!'

Fearsome's father said, 'I'm sorry, son: but your mother's right. We can't have a scandal, it wouldn't be fair to your mother or your brothers and sisters. So you've got to choose. Either do the right thing by this Princess and eat her, or else... or else you'll have to find somewhere else to live.'

'I wish you could meet her,' said Fearsome. 'I think you would like her.'

'We're too old to change,' said his father.

'And too wise!' snapped his mother. 'We know all about humans. They're heartless and greedy. She doesn't really love you, son. She can't. She's just using you.'

'All right,' said Fearsome, wiping away a tear. 'I'll go pack my bags.'

It was Fearsome the Dragon's saddest day. He flew to the Park carrying firewood in his jaws and a rucksack on his back with a few treasured belongings in it. He didn't tell the Princess about his parents, which he knew was wrong: but he couldn't bear to tell her what his parents thought of her. Nor could he bear for her to think unkind things about his parents, whom he loved.

He had some happy games that morning with the Princess and some lively discussions; then he spent the day pretending to be a scary dragon (it still didn't work and the princes still laughed at him) while the Princess lured another five princes up into the tower just by having long hair and looking pretty from a distance.

From time to time over the next week, Fearsome would look rather sad: but whenever the Princess asked what was wrong, he would say 'Nothing' grumpily (and perhaps a little guiltily) and change the subject.

This made the Princess angry, because she could tell something was going on: something Fearsome wasn't telling her. Yet she had told *him* all about *her* problems, such as her mother and father being lawn-mowered by Uncle Cheatalot. She and Fearsome got more and more annoyed with each other, until one day they had a fierce argument and said some rather mean things (which always makes the problem worse).

The last words of Princess Georgina were, 'So I'm not good enough to be your friend? Your parents throw you out and you don't even *tell* me? Why don't you go find someone you *like* and play Tonga with them instead?!'

'And *you* can go find someone else to boss around!' Fearsome roared before flying off to his own tower.

The danger

Neither of them knew about the telephone call the Witch had received at lunchtime.

'Hello. Baron Cheatalot here. Just checking on my dear little niece. Little … umm… I have her name written down somewhere… *George*. Is he – she – all right?'

The witch purred into the receiver at the other end. 'She's still locked in the Tower, if that's what you mean by "all right". Needs another pair of shoes, though. How these girls do run through shoes! That will cost you twenty gold pieces, plus tax of course.'

The Baron shouted down the phone. 'No!' he roared. 'No more shoes! No more ball gowns and trendy gym kit and pink wristwatches circled with diamonds!'

'What a shame,' said the witch coolly, smug in the certainty that the Baron didn't know that the only shoes she'd given the Princess was an old pair of cloth slippers. 'I'm afraid I can't look after her unless you pay for her Extras. I'll have to send her home, with a manly prince at her side and a hundred soldiers marching behind her, shouting "Long live Queen Georgina! Down with Baron Fatbelly!" Ha ha!'

'No!' shouted the Baron. 'That is not my name! And I'm sure she is called George and has a dog named Timmy! Or perhaps that was in a book I read…. No matter! I have had enough! The Princess turns twenty-one tomorrow and that is a Bad Thing. You must make sure she doesn't get a chance to blow out her birthday candles, or else…'

'Or else what?' taunted the witch.

'Or else there will be a lawnmower in your shower!'

The witch laughed down the phone. 'You don't scare me, Baron,' she said. 'But I *know* I scare you. Send me some money for the Princess's birthday, or you'll get a present you won't forget!'

The Baron slammed down the telephone and said several rude words like *Ztrrrngopod!* and *Sxmrcatrapp!* Then he sat and thought Bad Things for an hour. Then he smiled in a thoroughly evil manner and went to his dressing-up box.

That evening, Fearsome the Dragon turned off the pretend bonfire at the top of Dragon Mountain, sighed and read again the note from his mother:

Dear Fearsome, we do love you even though you've gone a little crazy. Sleep well and don't let the dragonflies bite. Your loving Ma (and your Pa). Dragon by Ara

He shed two steamy tears, then fell asleep hugging his teddy.

In the other tower, Princess Georgina was sitting on the cold stone floor, a pair of scissors in one hand and a looking glass in the other.

'Goodbye, hair!' she said sadly.

SNIP!

In a few minutes, she looked more like a boy than a girl. She tied one end of her hair to the pole in the middle of the roundabout. The rest of it she wrapped around the roundabout itself, with the far end free.

She too shed a couple of tears. Then she tucked herself into bed and fell asleep, planning to wake after the moon had gone down and then escape.

But someone else was waiting for the sky to darken. A few hours later, the Princess was awakened by the creaking of the door at the bottom of the tower. She heard a steady *clump clump clump* as someone climbed the stairs. All three hundred of them.

When the footsteps reached number two hundred, Georgina leaped from bed and dressed in her roughest clothes. She pulled at the free end of the spool of hair wrapped around the roundabout and flung it out the window, watching it slither almost to the ground. Then she seated herself on the window ledge, took hold of the hair and waited.

Whoever was outside the door was big and slow. He panted heavily as he pulled back the bolts and turned the doorknob. The door opened. A large, plump figure was lit by the dim starlight: one that looked familiar.

'Uncle Cheatalot!' she exclaimed.

'Ah! You are awake! What a shame!' he replied. 'It is

bad to have an unfortunate accident when you are awake! Come give your nice Uncle a hug, dear George!'

The Princess was no fool. 'Bye!' she shouted, and disappeared from the window. When Baron Cheatalot looked out, she was a quarter of the way down the tower already, sliding down her own hair.

Then she saw something flash in the starlight: her uncle's sword. She screamed.

Fearsome to the rescue

A hundred metres away, Fearsome the dragon was dozing. But in a moment he was wide awake and springing into the air.

The Princess! She's in trouble!

He flew towards the tower, but of course he could only see the back of it. At the front, the Baron was humming a happy Evil Baron tune while chopping through Georgina's hair. 'When the bough breaks,' he sang out, 'the cradle will fall! And down (*slice!*) will come Princess (*slice!*), cradle and all (*slice! slice!*). Ha ha!'

As he sang out *Ha ha!* the hair parted and the poor Princess began to fall like the cradle in the song, from halfway down the tower. She was destined for a nasty splat at the bottom and was rather sad about it...

... And then there was flapping of enormous wings

... and a rushing as of a mighty wind

... and a shout of Snap! Gotcha!

The Princess was seated on the dragon's back now; and he was speeding round and up towards the tower window, angry now as he had never been angry before.

The Baron saw him coming and pulled out his trusty bow and arrow and spear and grenade launcher and lawnmower, and hastily began loading them all ... just a little too late, for the dragon breathed out such a flame that the tower stones turned red with the heat, and then the whole tower tottered and fell, setting fire to the ride next door (the Hairy Rotter Doom Descent), which sent off its blazing roller coasters in all directions, making the Happy Kingdom a Towering Inferno and turning Slime City into a black, seething pool which spread and set light to the Marsh of Surprises and...

... Well, there wasn't much left in the morning when the witch came to open the Park. And when she made the mistake of stamping one diamond-studded knee-high boot in anger, the pavement cracked wide - and then wider - and then closed up suddenly a few seconds later, leaving nothing behind but the torn-off tip of a boot toe covered in pink diamonds.

Games forevermore

As for the Princess and the Dragon, they sped back to her own land, where the people cheered her as the New and Rather Nicer than Usual Queen. Fearsome set her down at the palace and prepared to fly off.

'Stay!' cried Queen Georgina. 'I mean, stay *please*, dear Fearsome. Unless of course you need to go home.'

'Haven't got a home,' said the dragon. 'Haven't got a job, either. My Mum will really shout at me for that... or she would if she was still talking to me.'

'Then stay with me. You can be my Dragon Consort. You're much better than a silly King.'

'You're much better than a plastic blow-up Princess.'

'Or a wind-up chicken?'

'As good as a toy rat.'

'A spinning strawberry?'

'A singing snake!'

'A bunny with a machine gun!'

'Snap!'

'Dragon!'

'... Yeah, I'll stay...'

And they played silly games happily ever after.

The Snow Queen

The voices

The Snow Queen's voice is clear and beautiful, with a hint of frost to it. She has the cool, self-assured sound of a woman who knows she's the most adored pop star on the planet. But every now and then she sounds puzzled: as if she suspects that being Important isn't the same as being happy or being good.

The Head Goblin has a deep, serious voice. You can tell he's the sort of guy who does his job without any fuss, and washes his sleigh once a month – which is when he washes himself, too.

Kay sounds gentle and a little dreamy. He's clearly a kind and thoughtful brother who wants to make Gerda happy – but he also wants to protect her from the Snow Queen. When he falls for the Snow Queen himself, his dreaminess takes over and his voice goes rather soft and soppy. This happens to men more often than you would suspect.

Gerda is bubbly and excitable, like a small, bouncy puppy. When you go to a music concert, she's the one you see right next to the stage, jumping up and down and squealing with delight. But when Kay is taken away, she becomes calm and purposeful, like a sensible guide dog. She's back to being bouncy again by the end.

The Troll is short and chunky, and has a low, chunky voice. He always sounds cheerful and happy. You can tell his happiness is something deep inside: it doesn't depend on other people telling him he's wonderful. Even sharing a cave with bats, bears and a bossy grandma makes him happy. His voice always sounds optimistic: as if he *knows* he'll win the love of the Snow Queen eventually, if she'll just give him a chance. (By the way, he does know his own name. He was pretending, to make the children laugh!)

The story

You may have read a very old story about a magic mirror that broke into a billion tiny pieces which were scattered about the world, finding their way into the hearts and eyes of people. Some of the fragments got stuck in books, turning them sour; others got into music that chills the soul or pictures that steal your happiness.

What you won't know is that the great-great-great-granddaughter of the wizard who made the mirror was the biggest Pop Star ever: the Snow Queen.

The Snow Queen was the most amazing performer in the world. She drove about in her magical sleigh, accompanied by a band of snow goblins. She sang the most wonderful songs, did the most beautiful dances and wore the most astonishing outfits. Her long hair swirled about; her crown sparkled; her clothes glittered; her fans cheered, wept and fainted.

She knew she could wiggle just one little finger and her fans would do anything she asked. She was the Greatest, and proud of it. Millions loved her and travelled across the world to the frozen lands she ruled, just to catch a glimpse of her. Children especially adored her, and she seemed to adore them... with the odd result that everywhere she went, children disappeared.

She "adopted" hundreds of these children, selecting them from the crowds that went to her concerts: and no one heard from them again. This didn't bother the children, who all longed to be the next child taken. It did annoy some parents however.

One of her biggest fans was a simple girl named Gerda who lived in a small apartment with her parents and her brother Kay. Kay didn't like the Snow Queen at all but he loved Gerda: so he didn't mind having the Snow Queen's pictures on all the walls of the house, and the Snow Queen's music pounding through his head all day. He even bought Gerda the latest album, The Snow Monster. And when he heard the Snow Queen was coming to their village, he saved his pocket money and bought tickets for the three nights of the show.

They joined the fans lining the snow-filled streets and cheered the beautiful Queen as she arrived in a huge red sleigh. She performed her Snow Monster concert dressed in red furs, wearing glittery red high heels and a bright red hat.

Gerda was entranced. And she was grateful to her brother Kay for making her wear a big red hat so that he could see her if they got separated in the crowd: for the hat's colour was just the same as the one the Snow Queen herself was wearing.

At the end of the concert, Gerda ran with Kay to the top of a little rise at the edge of the village and watched with a screaming, squealing press of Snow Queen fans as the Queen stepped into her carriage and was driven slowly through the streets.

Next to them was a short, broad, green Troll about their height, wearing some red boxer shorts… and nothing else, except a beaming smile.

'Hello,' said Kay and Gerda (they were very polite children).

'Hello!' said the Troll. 'Isn't she wonderful? I love her!'

'Me too!' sighed Gerda.

'I think she's phony,' said Kay. 'She pretends to be kind, but she's really selfish and proud.'

'No,' said the Troll. 'She's had a hard life and dat makes it difficult for her to be nice like you an' me. She just needs someone to love her an' look after her, an' den she'll be a greaaaat lady.'

Just then the Snow Queen's sleigh stopped opposite the little rise. She seemed to look across at Gerda, then turned to whisper something to the biggest of the goblins that trudged next to the sleigh. He nodded, then set off towards the tall red hat on the hill.

Kay saw the goblin stomping his way towards them: so he snatched the hat from Gerda's head, putting it on the Troll's rocky head instead. The goblin lurched up to the Troll, grabbed him with one big hand and tucked him under a large, brown, smelly armpit.

The sleigh had already left the village and was waiting just outside it, at a beauty spot overlooking a steep cliff. The head goblin marched up and dropped the Troll at the Snow Queen's feet.

The Queen raged at the goblin: 'What's this?!!'

The goblin bowed. 'Like you said, your Great Monsterness, the one with the red hat.'

'What? But this is an ugly Troll! I wanted a child!'

'This was the only one with a red hat, Majesty.'

The Queen looked at the Troll. Even wearing the red hat, he was scarcely shoulder high to her.

'Hello,' the Troll said. 'I love you!'

'You're crazy!' she exclaimed. 'Give me one reason why I shouldn't have you killed.'

The Troll thought. 'Uhh... because I want to marry you an' save you from all those borin' parties an' clubbin'. You can sing to me and Granny instead!'

'Granny? Who is Granny?'

'I live with Granny. You'll like her! Granny loves your songs. She says you got a nice big voice. Dat will help a lot, 'cause she don't hear too good. She has one of dem listening things like a musical instrument.'

'An ear trumpet, you mean?'

'No, bigger dan dat. She's got an ear *tuba*!'

The Snow Queen groaned. 'And you want me to leave my life of stardom and pleasure, just to look after your grandmother?'

'And do the cleanin',' said the Troll. 'Dere's lots of cleanin' 'cause it's a big cave, an' Granny's very messy.'

'A cave? I'm not living in a cave!'

The Troll said, 'But it's a nice cave! Except when the bears get in an' try to steal Granny's chocolate. Dey makes a lot of mess, dem bears. Worse dan the wildcats.

Not as messy as the bats, though.'

'Bears? Cats?! Bats?!!'

'Yeah an' it's even better dan dat! We got a television too! It only gets one channel, but dat's the Music Channel, which is how we saw you. Granny says I gotta find me a wife: an' you is the only one for me!'

The Snow Queen kicked the Troll, hard.

'Owwwwww!' she said. 'I think I've broken my toe!' She sat on the ground, clutching her left foot. She took off her left red high heel and threw the shoe at the Troll.

'Thank you!' he exclaimed. 'Dat's a nice gift for our first date! Ohhhh… Does your foot hurt? Let me kiss it better for you!'

He knelt and gave her foot a gentle kiss.

'Oh!' she said quietly, because it was surprisingly nice to have her foot kissed by a troll.

But she was also very, very offended: so she shouted to her goblin guards, 'Take him away! Throw him down the mountain!'

… The Troll bounced to the bottom of the mountain with the shoe clutched to his chest and a big smile on his face.

'She loves me!' he sighed. 'She gave me her shoe!'

For the second day of the concert, Kay made his sister wear a big green hat. And again she was happy, because this time the Snow Queen was wearing a wonderful emerald green outfit. The Queen slithered to and fro across the sea-green stage like a hypnotic, sinuous snake: and the mesmerised eyes of her fans followed her left and right, like the eyes of a mouse trapped in a corner by a cobra.

The Snow Queen did have one problem: it was hard to dance with a big green ankle brace on her left foot.

Afterwards, Kay and Gerda stood again on the little rise at the edge of the village. The same Troll was there, wearing Gerda's red hat from the day before (with a lot of snow on it) and the Snow Queen's red high heel shoe… and green boxer shorts this time.

'I know you!' said the Troll. 'You gave me dis hat. You is my friends!'

They shook hands and asked about each other's families, as is the custom.

'Granny is very deaf an' shouts a lot an' throws things at me. But I love her!' said the Troll. 'What about you?'

Kay said, 'We're very well and nobody shouts at us, or throws anything.'

Gerda said, 'But it's boring at home. Nothing happens. I wish I could go live with the Snow Queen instead.'

The Troll said, 'I could send my Granny to visit you. Dat would make it exciting!'

Kay suddenly noticed something. He pointed at the Troll's foot. 'Isn't that one of the Snow Queen's shoes?' he asked excitedly. 'It's so beautiful!'

'Yes, she gave it to me. Den she had me thrown down a mountain, so I had to climb back up it. Dat was difficult to do with one high heel on!'

Gerda asked, 'Why did she have you thrown down the mountain? She's so kind and wonderful: I don't believe she would ever hurt anyone!'

The Troll said, 'She wants me to go away, but I want to be wid her forever. Dat's good, 'cause opposites attract. It means she loves me!'

'No, it doesn't,' said Kay. 'It means she *doesn't* love you. If she loved anyone, she would love a boy like me.'

An odd, dreamy look came into Kay's eyes as he said this. He added, 'You two are too different from each other. Birds of a feather flock together, you know.'

The Troll shook his head. 'I'm not a bird,' he said. 'I'm the opposite of a bird, dat's why we attract!'

Just then, the Snow Queen passed by the hill they were standing on. Everyone waved excitedly. The Queen saw Gerda up there, dressed in green, hopping with excitement and waving madly, her big green hat flapping up and down.

The Queen smiled and leaned out of the sleigh to talk to the head goblin. He nodded his head.

'The green hat, your Majesty? You're sure this time?'

'Of course I'm sure!' she hissed.

The goblin stomped off again. Kay saw him coming

and swapped the Troll's red hat for Gerda's green one. Once again, the goblin tucked the Troll under a smelly armpit and lugged him back to the sleigh.

'What??? You?!!!' the Snow Queen roared.

'I love you, Snow Queen!'

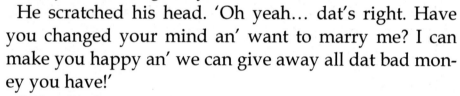

'You're the same ugly Troll as last night! And I hate you now as much as I did then!'

The Troll said, 'How did you know I was the same troll? I got a green hat on dis time!'

'But you've also got my red shoe on!'

He scratched his head. 'Oh yeah... dat's right. Have you changed your mind an' want to marry me? I can make you happy an' we can give away all dat bad money you have!'

'What bad money?'

'You make too much money. No one needs lots of money, it only makes dem sad. You can make lots of poor children happy wid your money instead!'

The Snow Queen shouted, 'You're crazy!' She aimed a second kick at the Troll, using her right foot this time.

'Owwww!' I've hurt my other toe!'

She fell to the ground, clutching her right foot. She tore off her green high heel and threw it at the Troll. It bounced off his hard little head, but he caught it before it fell to the ground.

'You've given me a present for our second date!' he exclaimed. 'You must *really* love me!'

'No!' she roared. 'I hate you! You're ugly!'

'Thank you!'

'And stupid! And so *ordinary*!'

'Thank you!'

'And green!'

'Thank – Hey, who are you callin' green?'

'You!' She tried to kick him again. 'Ouch! Oh, my foot really hurts!'

'I'll kiss it better!' The Troll bent and kissed the Snow Queen's right foot.

'Oh!' she said quietly, because it was rather nice. But then she shouted, 'Leave me alone!'

'No,' he said. 'I can't do dat. I love you an' I'm gonna make you reeeeally happy!'

'I *am* happy!'

'Granny says you can't be happy, cos you ain't got a nice cave to clean an' a nice Troll husband an' little children to play wid.'

'I *am* happy!'

'Not yet!'

The Snow Queen ordered her goblins to throw the Troll down the biggest, steepest cliff they could find. Then she drove her sleigh home and had three parties on the same night, just to prove how happy she was.

The third night of the concert was the loudest and longest. The Snow Queen arrived in a blue sleigh and was dressed in an electric blue outfit, with both feet bandaged in fluorescent blue tape. But she was a true performer and her injured feet didn't stop her from dancing and singing beautifully.

Gerda was dressed all in floaty blue silks, with a huge blue hat on her head. She sang along with all the songs (she knew them by heart), did all the dance moves (ditto) and made Snow Monster signs and patterns with her arms and hands (ditto ditto).

At the end of the concert, they gathered again on the little rise at the edge of the village. They looked around for the little Troll, but he was nowhere to be seen.

When the Snow Queen passed by the hill they were standing on, she saw Gerda up there dressed in blue, hopping with excitement and waving, her big blue hat flapping about like a demented bluebird.

The Queen leaned out of the sleigh to talk to the head goblin. He asked doubtfully, 'The blue hat, your Majesty? You're sure? I mean, the last two times -'

'Of course I'm sure!' she hissed.

The goblin stomped off again. Kay saw him coming and... and...

.... And the dreamy look came into Kay's eyes again, and he took Gerda's blue hat from her head and put it on his own head.

The goblin tucked Kay under a brown, smelly armpit and lugged him back to the sleigh.

'What??? You?!!!' the Snow Queen roared. 'I wanted -'

But then she bent closer and looked into Kay's eyes. 'This is a most interesting boy,' she said. 'I think he might do...'

Just then the Troll turned up, looking rather tired and nearly falling over every few steps because was wearing high heels of two different heights and colours.

'Sorry I'm late!' he called. 'Dat was a biiiiigggg mountain you threw me down! And it's hard to climb back up when you're wearin' high heels!'

'I thought I'd got rid of you!' groaned the Queen.

'Oh... Does dat mean you was worried about me?'

'No! It means I hoped you were dead!'

'You got a funny way of showin' your love! But I don't mind. When we're married and sittin' side by side in the cave holdin' hands, it will be alllllll right!'

The Snow Queen stamped her feet (*Ouch!*) and shouted, 'I don't want to live in a cave! I spent years fighting my way up to stardom, and I'm not going back! Look, you ignorant little rock-cruncher, when I was a child I lived in a trailer park, in a small, dirty trailer. We had *nothing* – not even a television! I had only one pair of shoes then: now I've got a thousand!'

'Oh.' The Troll thought hard, his little forehead wrinkling. 'But when you was a little girl in the trailer, wasn't you happy? Wasn't it the best time of your life?'

'Of course not, you *idiot!*' The Snow Queen felt in a secret pocket of her sparkling blue rubbery monster outfit and pulled out something she rarely had to use these days: a magic wand that had belonged to her great-great-great-grandfather.

She raised it high into the air and prepared to blast the Troll to smithereens with some rather nasty magic. But she stopped, horrified by a sudden thought:

She had been very happy in the trailer park, playing with her brother and sister and ugly mongrel dog named Bella. She had sung from sheer happiness back in those distant days....

'Take *that!*' she shouted and waved the wand at the Troll. He was turned into a rather ugly block of ice wearing high heels. The block teetered on its unmatched heels and fell onto its side. It lay there on the snowy ground, and snowflakes from the sky began to cover it. The Snow Queen's sleigh sped away …

While Kay was being driven across snowbound lands towards the distant palace of the Queen, Gerda was pushing through the crowds, calling for him.

She came to the place where the Snow Queen's sleigh had rested outside the village; but all that was left of Kay was a floppy blue hat, half-buried in the snow.

She sat upon an icy rock holding the hat, and began to cry. She realised that the Snow Queen wasn't so wonderful after all: her brother Kay was more important to her than a hundred songs or a thousand glittery shoes. She remembered all the things they had done together, and his kindness, and the way he laughed, and… well, all those good things you miss when someone has gone and you can't get them back.

Her tears fell onto the cold, cold rock she was sitting on. And maybe there was something magic in her tears, or maybe all honest tears have a little magic in them, because something happened to the rock.

It melted. It cracked. It fell to pieces beneath her, and she went sprawling upon the snowy ground. When she got to her feet, she saw the little Troll freeing himself from the last bonds of ice and trying to stand up. She took his hand and helped him to his feet.

'I know you!' he exclaimed. 'You're wid dat nice boy named after a letter of the alphabet!'

Gerda said, 'You mean my brother Kay. Will...will you help me? I want to find Kay.'

'I like Kay,' said the Troll. 'He's my friend. He gave me two hats! But the Snow Queen took him away.'

'Oh no!' cried Gerda. 'I'll never see him again!'

The Troll patted her kindly on the shoulder. 'Of course you will,' he said. 'When the Snow Queen comes to live with me and Granny, she can bring him to the cave an' you can come get him!'

'We need to find them *now*,' said Gerda. 'Before something terrible happens to him.'

'All right,' said the Troll. 'Let's go right away, den!' And he began walking off.

'Wait,' said Gerda. 'You can't go dressed like that!'

'Why not?' asked the Troll, looking down.

He was wearing one green high heeled shoe, a much higher red shoe, Gerda's green hat from yesterday and a pair of blue boxer shorts.

'For a start, nothing matches!'

'I could take off the boxer shorts.... But den I would be very cold.'

Their quest took them across great snowy mountains and down into a snowy valley. Sometimes the Troll carried Gerda on his back, and once she tried to carry him (it didn't work and they both fell off a cliff). They argued all the way about the Snow Queen.

Gerda would say things like, 'She's the most horrible woman in history! She's evil! And selfish! And a liar!

She just *pretends* to have a heart!'

The Troll would shake his head. 'All she needs is true love and some good books to read. We got one at home about my lion friend Aslan. She'll like dat one!'

The Snow Queen's palace

Meanwhile, Kay was hard at work. When he arrived at the Queen's palace, he'd been given a hundred tests to discover what he was good at. When the Snow Queen found that he was brilliant at creating music videos, she clapped her hands… and had him chained to a desk where he slaved all day at a computer screen.

All the Queen's "children" were connected to the most amazing computer network in the world, the Blizzard. They had circular SnowPads to carry around with them: a combination of phone, camera, music centre, pizza maker and task monitor, with an inbuilt tracking device so that the Snow Queen knew where her workers were and what they were doing.

All the children in the Snow Palace had jobs. Some wrote the Snow Queen's songs. Some composed her music. Some designed or sewed her dresses. Others invented her dances. Most of them had to do some cooking and cleaning. And all of them had the job of telling her how Wonderful she was. *W Time*, they called it.

There was a *W Time* rota built into the calendar of every SnowPad. This told you when it was your turn to go up to the Snow Queen and say something like:

You're snoooooow special!
I think you're amazing!
You rock awesomely!
I'm so happy you chose me!
Snow monsters rule!

… But if someone was late for *W Time*, or didn't say something the Queen liked, or didn't say it as if they meant it, then… well… you see…

… Actually, I don't want to tell you what happened to them. But it was even worse than being carried around under the head goblin's armpit.

Surprisingly, they thought they were the luckiest children in the world. I suppose that's because of the tiny specks of magic mirror glass stuck in their eyes: they just didn't see straight or think straight or feel straight. All they could see was the awesomeness of the Queen.

But they were better off than the Snow Queen herself, because she had a big piece of mirror glass stuck in her heart. She felt nothing at all, *nothing*: except how important she was. Whenever she began to feel the tiniest bit guilty about this, she cured that by looking in her mirror and saying firmly to her reflection: *I'm worth it!*

As for Gerda, her speck of glass had been washed out of her eye when she cried remorsefully for Kay. And the Troll wasn't affected by the glass at all. He was just foolishly in love with a heartless woman. That sort of thing happens a lot.…

Kay's videos got better every day. He invented the SQH – the Snow Queen Hologram. The SQH was a 3D image created by crossing the light from three lasers above a stage. It looked so like the Snow Queen herself that some of her workers accidentally spent their *W Time* telling the SQH how wonderful she was instead of telling the real Queen, and so they suffered the horrible punishment of… no, I still can't bear to tell you.

Meanwhile, Gerda and the Troll were crossing the desolate steppes, waist deep in snow. They met reindeer, robber girls and other fanciful creatures you would expect in a Snow Queen story: but they ignored them all and pressed on. Well, actually, they did have reindeer stew a few times…

'I wish we had Chili pepper popcorn instead,' said the Troll as they walked on. 'Dat's about the best thing in the world! Chili popcorn and a biggggg bottle of cola!'

'I'd prefer a steaming mug of cocoa,' said Gerda.

'Oh,' said the Troll. 'Maybe we should ask at dat big snow castle place up ahead…'

So they did… and were immediately thrown into the Snow Queen's dungeons…. where there wasn't a drop of cocoa or kernel of popcorn to be seen.

The next day, they were taken before the Queen. She was sitting in her Judgement Room with hundreds of her workers gathered about her. One of them was Kay; he looked at Gerda, but didn't know her. The speck of glass distorted everything he looked at, and his mind was full of the Snow Queen.

Gerda and the Troll were led forward to stand before the Queen. The Troll was still wearing the Queen's mismatched high heels, and some children started to giggle until an icy, Queenly glance silenced them.

'Names!' ordered one of the guards.

'Gerda,' said Gerda.

'Oh yeah,' said the Troll, pulling a piece of paper from his boxer shorts pocket. 'I thought I might need dat, so I got Granny to write it down for me before I set out. Here it is… Oh.'

He stared at the paper for a long time.

'Well: *what is it?*' shouted the Snow Queen.

'I don't know,' he said. 'I can't read.'

'Arrrrgh!' exclaimed the Queen angrily, slapping the arm of her throne chair in a fit of annoyance. But all around her, the children started to giggle again. They tried to stop themselves, but couldn't.

'Take the paper from him and read it out!' she ordered the guard, who snatched the paper, stared at it and shook his head.

'It's a jumble of meaningless scribbles, your Snow Monsterness,' he said.

'Arrrrgh!' exclaimed the Queen again, slapping the *other* arm of her throne chair.

The children giggled even more. Some of their faces were turning red with the effort of holding it in.

'Why has she written scribbles?' she asked the Troll.

'*Now* I remember,' said the Troll. 'Granny can't write!'

'Arrrrgh!' exclaimed the Queen for a third time, beating on *both* arms of her chair until they broke. Around her, the children were roaring with laughter. Some of them had to sit on the floor, helpless with mirth.

'It's *not* funny!' shouted the Snow Queen. She asked the Troll, 'What's your grandmother's name, then?'

'Uh… Granny?'

'No! What do her friends call her?'

'Mean old lady!'

'Arrrrgh! What did your Grandpa call her?'

'*Very* mean old lady!'

By now, the children were laughing so hard that they had tears in their eyes. Even the Snow Queen was starting to smile a little.

'And is this the same mean old lady you want me to go and clean for?' she asked.

The Troll exclaimed, 'Yes! Den if you dance an' sing for her, dat might make her happy! An' maybe the bears would be happy too. Dey fight a lot wid each other. And wid the mountain lions. And wid Granny.'

Now everyone had tears rolling down their face, apart from the Queen. Somewhere in the crowd, Kay wiped his eyes and looked again at the two figures standing in front of the Queen. *Gerda!!!* he thought.

The Queen asked the Troll, 'Why doesn't your Granny do the cleaning?'

'She's too busy wrestling wid the lions and bears. She usually wins, too!'

'W-w-why don't *you* do the cleaning then?' asked the Snow Queen, who was trying very hard not to laugh but couldn't stop a sudden fit of giggles.

The Toenail Fairy

The Troll said, 'I do some! But it's very difficult to mop when the bears are tryin' to bite your leg off. Besides, I got a job. I help my Uncle. He's *very* important.'

'And what does he do?'

'He's the Toenail Fairy!'

At this point, the Snow Queen began to laugh as freely as the children. (The children who laughed the hardest were those who had read *Wicked Tales Two* and knew what the Toenail Fairy did with the toenails).

The Troll continued, 'And when I'm not helping Uncle Robin or tellin' stories at schools, I dig for jewels in the mountain. I've found three so far! You could come help me dig, an' we could give the money to poor children!'

The Snow Queen was suddenly angry again. 'I do quite enough charity work!' she exploded. 'And I'm not scrabbling about in the dirt for *anyone*.'

She took a deep breath and counted to ten before proclaiming her judgement:

'Take him out and put him in the mirror!'

There was a gasp from the children.

The guards led the Troll out of the hall… along a dark corridor… out onto the snow-covered hillside… along an icy path… to a big, hollowed-out, dazzling bowl of light in the snow.

It was a mirror. A silvery, curving mirror as big as your playground, throwing back the light of the sky, with a billion glittering ice crystals dancing above it.

The children had all trooped out to see the Troll's punishment, but were hanging back: they didn't want to get too close to the mirror.

The Snow Queen put her hand on the Troll's shoulder and pushed him forward to the edge of the mirror. As she did this, Gerda (who was still held by a guard) felt a hand slip into her own. She turned her head and saw Kay behind her. He put a finger to his lips: *Quiet!*

The Queen proclaimed, 'My great-great-great-grand-father made a magic mirror of enormous power. But when the winged monkey-goblins were flying it across the skies, it shattered into a billion pieces. Now I've re-built it! And I've made it out of the strongest, most important thing I know. What do you think that is?'

'Uh… professional wrestlers?' asked the Troll.

'No!'

'Den it must be Love. Dat's strong and important.'

'No!' shouted the Snow Queen. 'I've built the mirror out of my own Fame. As my celebrity has grown, so my mirror has spread and deepened. It is great and beautiful, and terrible to look upon.'

'Like a bigggg monster,' said the Troll.

'Yes! A beautiful Fame Monster. And whoever looks into my mirror will fall in love with me and do whatever I ask. I will become the greatest person on earth, and the power of the mirror will grow, fan by loving fan.'

She smiled triumphantly.

'But you don't need a big mirror to make people love you,' said the Troll. 'No one does.'

'Silence!' she commanded. 'Those who refuse to look into the mirror will be *thrown* into it, and will slide down into the dark hole at its centre and become part of the mirror itself. Ha! I win both ways!'

She pushed him forward to the edge of the mirror and commanded him to look into it.

He said. 'I won't look. I don't need to, because I love you anyway! And I don't think you're really bad. I think you just need a hug. And a new mop.'

The Queen was just about to order her guards to throw the Troll into the mirror… when Kay pressed a button on his SnowPad.

An image of the Snow Queen – the Snow Queen Hologram, the SQH - appeared at the side of the mirror, laughing and dancing. She looked so happy and carefree that it made the children smile and start to dance as well. Then the SQH spread her arms and stepped onto the mirror. The image seemed to be wearing ice skates, for the SQH went gliding merrily across the large mirror, singing joyfully and doing a glorious Snow Monster Dance as she skated.

All the children were cheering the SQH; none of them were looking at the real Snow Queen any longer.

How could they?! For a moment the Queen was filled with rage at the children. She reached for her wand, preparing to blast them all to cinders.

But she paused when she heard Gerda's puzzled voice, as the girl looked from the happy skating hologram who seemed to love everybody, to the cold, angry woman who wanted everybody to love her:

'Which one is the real Snow Queen?'

Kay answered, 'The one she decides to be.'

The Troll said stubbornly, 'She's the one with a heart. I know she is.' He looked into the mirror, and his eyes went funny. He took a step forward, then another. Then he too slid down into the bowl shaped mirror.

He was wearing one green high heeled shoe and one red one of a different height. He tottered to and fro as he slid but managed to stay upright. His heels made a screeching, grating sound as they dug into the glassy top of the mirror, slicing it into ribbons as he spiralled around and down, around and up and around and...

Above him, the children laughed even louder.

But the Snow Queen was furious. *He was ripping her*

lovely mirror to shreds! She was hopping mad – literally. She hopped so hard that she too slipped off the edge and went skating down on her Snow Queen platform shoes, ripping the mirror in quite a different pattern.

The Troll skated past her, shouting, 'Isn't dis fun?!'

'No it isn't!' she hissed back. 'It's terrible!'

But then she started laughing. It was the most wonderful fun she'd ever had, apart from those happy years as a child in the trailer park. She leaned forward and skated faster, faster, faster, until she caught up with the Troll and flew past him.

'Ha!' she cried. 'Can't catch me!'

'Yes I can!' he shouted back.

And they started a wild, hilarious chase after the SQH, ripping the magic mirror into tiny slivers which melted in the sunlight and ran down into the dark hole at the centre, blocking it up and leaving only a lovely glassy surface for the children to skate down....

Granny's Cave

If you skip forward a few months, you'll see a rather happy cave that's full of song and dance and mopping. Even Granny seems pleased, and the bears do more salsa dancing than wrestling these days.

The Snow Palace children have been sent home, but they use their SnowPads to keep in touch with the Snow Queen and one another. They still do most of her songwriting, dressmaking, stage design and so on: but they get paid for it now.

The Snow Queen has given away most of her money to help children around the world, and doesn't miss a penny of it. She spends a lot of time visiting schools and hospitals; the trolls tell stories and she sings songs.

She still does a concert each Saturday, but she gives all the money to charity. And whenever the Snow Queen hasn't managed to get the cleaning done to Granny's satisfaction and is grounded for the weekend, she just laughs and sends a Snowmail to Kay, who arranges for the SQH to do her Saturday concert instead.

She and the Troll spend Sundays digging for jewels, though they rarely find any. Afterwards the Snow Queen sits at home in the cave, holding hands with the Troll. They laugh while they eat chili pepper, garlic, lime and curry popcorn, drink cola and watch the Music Channel on TV. Then the Snow Queen throws popcorn at the Troll, he sprays her with cola, and the bears and wildcats come out from the kitchen and do a little wrestling with everyone while the Snow Queen sings her latest hit.

Bliss!

Sleeping Beauty feat. 7EB

The voices (get your dictionary out now!)

Prince Credulous sounds humble, affable and candid. You can tell he's a friendly guy who doesn't lie, doesn't pretend to be better than he is, never sneers at others and won't try to fool you. Because he's honest, he assumes everyone else is like that too: so you *know* that a lot of people will take advantage of him.

Princess Mendacious is so beautiful, clever and eloquent that everyone believes what she says. She talks with what sounds like affection; but it's actually affectation. The only clue to this is that her voice is a tiny bit too smooth and self-satisfied.

The Easter Bunnies aren't as loud as usual. You can still think of them as a gang of US Marines or CSI cops, but this time imagine they've gone under cover and are pretending to be serious musicians on a concert tour... that is, until they open the violin cases and take out their chainsaws.

Little Beauty sounds excessively sweet. She probably lisps a little. When she giggles, you can imagine her golden curls bouncing around her shoulders. Grown-ups think she's sooooooo cute.

Her sister **Princess Duty** has a rebellious teenage voice, as if she's angry at the world and especially at her boring parents and annoying little sister. Her friend the **Horse** has a playful whinny.

The various **Witches** cackle a lot, which is a dead giveaway but they really don't care. They **like** being witches and **adore** doing nasty, witchy, maleficent things to people. If you have a problem with that, you'd better keep quiet. Or find a good dictionary.

The **Kings and Queens** know that they are far superior to the rest of us, and they *sound* like they know it.

The story (you will need a dictionary...!)

From Wicked Tales Three: *About a mile away, an old witch was pronouncing the baby Princess's doom at her Christening Party. 'When little Beauty is ten years old,' she croaked, 'she will prick her finger on a... on a...' She looked up into the sky, her mouth open in surprise. '... a carrot???' she asked wonderingly as an orange pointy vegetable dropped towards her and then made a hole in her black hat... and in her head.*

... Almost ten years later and in a kingdom not far from little Beauty's, Prince Credulous was worrying. But surely, you'll say, he had nothing to worry about:

👑 He was the richest prince for miles around (kilometres hadn't been invented yet).

👑 The King and Queen said they adored him.

👑 He had hundreds of friends, whose names he had written in a book with a drawing of each face: he called them his face book friends.

👑 He was engaged to a tall, blond, absolutely gorgeous princess. Their wedding was only a week away.

But he *was* worried. So he went to visit his betrothed, the wonderful Princess Mendacious, who was at a party as usual and surrounded by rich friends and admirers as usual (she had a *thousand* friends in her book!). Though she didn't really know them, she was chattering away to them as if she did: this would be called *tweeting*, if that had been invented yet.

According to an old legend, all princesses are given the choice of being beautiful, clever and good: but they're only allowed two out of three. Princess Mendacious was gloriously beautiful and amazingly clever; but Prince Credulous thought she *must* be good as well, because she always smiled at him so kindly.

'Princess,' he said to her now, 'I'm rich and famous and royal. But what if I wasn't? Would I still have all my friends? And… and would you still love me?'

'You silly boy! Of course I would!' she laughed, kissing his cheek. Then she added quickly, 'But – you *are* rich and famous and so on, aren't you?'

'Why, yes,' said the Prince.

'Good!' said the Princess. 'Then it's one of those silly questions they call rhetorical – or theoretical – or hypothetical – or even parabolic. Which means that the answer doesn't really matter.'

'You're so clever!' said the Prince. 'And beautiful! And you *must* be good as well, because you're kind even to bad people like my evil cousin, Count Usurper. I saw you dancing sweetly with him last week, even though you say you dislike him.'

'Ah yes,' said the Princess. 'Usurper is rather handsome, but he's very naughty and *not* rich, so I don't like him at all. He *isn't* rich like you, is he?'

'He has scarcely a penny.'

'It wouldn't matter if he *was* rich,' proclaimed the Princess. 'You're the man for me! I wouldn't marry Count Usurper for all the artichokes in Andalusia, the beetroot in Belarus, the cherries in China, the -'

'I get the picture,' said the Prince and went home happy. Except...

Except that he made the mistake of wishing out loud as he passed an old cottage inhabited by the three daughters of the witch who was carroted in *Wicked Tales Three*. He said to his horse, 'I wish – I *so* wish I could find out for sure who my real friends are.'

The horse said nothing. But the witches in the cottage cackled to one another before the eldest shouted out the window: 'Granted!' She pulled out her wand and concocted a cruel little spell then and there.

But she should have thought of this: when bad people try to hurt good people, they sometimes end up hurting themselves most.

The next morning, something terrible occurred. The ancient nurse who had helped bring baby Credulous into the world turned up at the Palace and whispered a dark secret to the King and Queen: twenty years ago, there had been a dreadful mix-up in the Royal Hospital. Their true son was Usurper; Credulous was only...

'...An imposter?' asked Princess Mendacious when she was told the news later that day. 'A mountebank, charlatan and counterfeit?'

'Sadly so,' said the King. 'He'll have to go, of course.'

'Good! I never really liked him,' said Princess Mendacious. 'He was such a boring do-gooder. Always trying to help the poor, and silly things like that.'

'Exactly,' agreed the Queen. 'When he was a child, he tried to invent Easter eggs so he could share them! I *knew* there must be something wrong with him.'

'He was never properly *Kingly*,' said the King. 'Not like Usurper is.'

Princess Mendacious said thoughtfully, 'I've always loved Count Usurper, by the way...'

And so Credulous was asked to leave the palace, while a laughing Usurper took over his rooms, his servants and even his friends. New wedding invitations were sent out, proclaiming the undying love between Usurper and Mendacious.

Poor ex-Prince Credulous quickly found out who his friends were. He got in touch with all the friends in his face book and found that a third of them didn't know who he was, a third said they'd never liked him anyway and the rest just ignored him.

The common people still treated him with respect; and he had a few good friends who stayed loyal to him. He was sitting with them now in a quiet bar, drinking carrot cocktails.

'I'm so grateful to have four friends left,' he said.

'Seven,' said one of his friends.

'Of course,' he said. He counted them again. There were only four of them and they were clearly bunnies: but wasn't going to upset his only friends in the world by arguing about numbers.

He said, 'Everyone else abandoned me when they learned I wasn't really a prince.'

Bunny Seven twitched his ears. 'What?' he asked. 'You mean you used to be a prince? Oh. So that's why you was always wearin' that crown thingy.'

The other bunnies sighed and shook their heads. Seven wasn't the sharpest carrot in the cake.

Ex-Prince Credulous continued sadly, 'They liked me when I was rich and famous, but no one wants to know me now. Even Princess Mendacious has forgotten she loves me –'

Bunny Seven's ears twitched again. 'What? Mendacious is a girl?'

'Of course,' said the Prince.

'Ah. That explains all the kissin', then,' said Seven.

The Prince sighed, 'Now she kisses Usurper, not me!'

The Bunnies made sympathetic noises and ordered another round of drinks: eight carrot cocktails.

'You ought to leave the kingdom,' said the Head Bunny (Bunny 4, as you may have guessed). 'Why not join us?'

'Yeah. Come with us!' the others urged.

'– We're going to fight oppression!'

'– No, it's depression we're fighting!'

'– Repression.'

'– First impressions.'

'We're the BCIS!

'– Nah, we're the CSI-B!'

'– B-CBI!'

'– I tawt I taw a puddy tat!'

The others turned and looked at Bunny Seven.

He said, 'Uh... wrong TV show. Sorry.'

'TV?' asked Credulous.

'Don't worry about it. It hasn't been invented yet.'

'Oh,' said Credulous. 'Like Easter eggs, you mean? Mummy wouldn't let me invent those. I thought it would be lovely to have egg-shaped chocolate you gave to your friends to eat.'

'To **shoot**, you mean!' said all the Bunnies at once.

'No, to *eat*. That's what you do with chocolate.'

'You're weird,' said the Head Bunny. 'But we like you. Anyway, we've given up shooting chocolate Easter eggs for Lent. No more guns! But we don't need them. We've got other protection.'

He nodded at a pile of violin cases stacked by the bar.

'Violins? You fight with music?' asked the Prince.

'Nah: we've invented something even scarier than violins. Hey – we can lend you one if you join us.'

Credulous exclaimed, 'I'll do it! I'd do anything to stop me thinking about that false-hearted Princess!'

'Her name was a clue, though,' said Bunny Seven.

'What?' asked the other Bunnies.

'*Mendacious*. Means tellin' lots of lies.'

They all stared at Bunny Seven. The Head Bunny said, 'This isn't like you. Are you ill?'

Seven shook his head. 'Nah.' He reached into his bunny rucksack and took out a book. 'I've invented a dictionary,' he said. He showed the ex-Prince the definition of "Mendacious" and then "Usurper".

'And you'll never guess what Credulous means!' he added. He turned some pages.

'Oh. I see,' said the ex-Prince. 'I trust people too easily. Oh dear. My middle name is now Regret.'

'Gullible, more like,' suggested a Bunny.

'Nah,' said Seven, turning to another page. 'I got it here: Pathetic.'

In the Kingdom of Sleeping Beauty

'When little Beauty is ten years old, she will prick her finger on a... carrot???'

The King and Queen took the threat seriously, even though the evil witch hadn't survived the carrot missile. And so Beauty had to be protected from carrots.

Carrots were not allowed within the Royal City, and possession of a carrot was punishable by Broccoli Soup (which you had to eat cold).

The use of the word "carrot" was banned within the palace grounds. They were now referred to as Orange Pointy Vegetables.

As the Princess's 10th birthday approached, her parents became more worried than ever: so they advertised for a bodyguard for Beauty. Auditions for *Kingdom's Got Carrots* were held in the palace in front of an invited audience, with a celebrity judging panel of carrot experts including farmers, chefs and a horse who had wandered in by mistake.

Many competitors performed on stage, showing how they would protect the Princess from evil carrots. But no one was good enough. It was Thumbs Down, and then Down to the Dungeons. Finally, the master of ceremonies announced the arrival of:

'The band 7EB! With their conductor, the Artist Formerly Known as Prince Credulous!'

Four creatures with long ears, fluffy tails and seven violin cases climbed onto the stage. They opened their cases and took out… seven chainsaws.

While the Bunnies were tuning up their chainsaws, Credulous set up a conductor's podium and got out his wooden baton. At a nod from the Head Bunny, he bowed to the panel of judges and the audience.

'We present to you… *A Symphony of Destruction*… performed by 7EB!'

'The Seven Easter Bunnies!' shouted one Bunny.

'Yeah, that's us!'

'With our weapons of mass destruction!'

'Which we invented because they sound better than violins, and cut through wood as well!'

Credulous tapped his baton twice on the podium. The Bunnies launched their roaring chainsaws into the air, caught them, threw them to each other, balanced them on their noses, on the horse's nose, bounced them off the floor, off the ceiling, off the horse's rump: sometimes with all seven saws in the air at once.

Then Credulous slid furniture in their direction, directing the Symphony of Destruction with his baton. Chairs, tables and grand pianos were sliced into pretty patterns, ground into sawdust or formed into wooden dragons, toy dogs and dolls' houses before the delighted eyes of the audience.

'And now,' proclaimed Credulous. 'We'll show you how we would handle the threat of marauding Parrots!'

He unveiled a large cage of squawking and rather worried parrots. He reached inside and took one out, preparing to hurl it into the maelstrom of spinning, buzzing, flying chainsaws.

'Wait!' shouted a voice. It was the King.

A chainsaw clattered to the floor and began chewing a hole in it. Six others followed.

The King said sternly, 'Not parrots… *carrots*!'

Someone whispered in the King's ear. He corrected himself: 'I mean, orange pointy vegetables!'

'Wait a minute,' said one of the Bunnies. 'Carrots? Who'd want to hurt a carrot? I mean, carrots are great. Carrots are full of good stuff. Right?'

The horse whinnied at this. The other judges turned to look at him, and he hung his head guiltily.

'Carrots must be sliced and diced,' said a chef.

'Carrots are the root of all evil,' said a farmer.

'Carrots are a threat to the kingdom,' said the King.

'*I love them!*' exclaimed a new voice.

There was a gasp. Then the Queen rose and pointed an angry finger at an unusual young woman sitting in the audience.

'Go to your room, Princess Duty!'

'But Mother –'

'Immediately!' thundered the Queen.

The Princess flounced away, eating what looked like an orange pointy vegetable. Prince Credulous stared at her as she stomped past. He'd never seen a princess like her, with her short, spiky red hair, pink steel-toed work boots and a t-shirt that read *"Daddy's little nightmare"*.

Duty was the twenty year old sister of Beauty. As you know, princesses can be beautiful, clever and good, but only two out of the three. Duty was not beautiful. She had a face like the back end of something that hadn't been invented yet. She was definitely good: she even helped old ladies cross the road when they didn't want to go. No one knew whether she was clever. However, coming out as a carrot lover just before her sister's 10th birthday wasn't wise.

'That's enough!' thundered the King. Then he asked sternly, 'Does anyone else here like carrots?'

The horse wasn't wise either. He held up one hoof. The King scowled at him.

'Anyone *else*?' hissed the King.

The horse held up a second hoof. Then he fell over.

The Bunnies looked at one another. One of them said, 'We've – uh – had experience of carrots.'

'– Yeah! We know them inside and out!'

'– Mostly inside.'

'– Not that we *like* them, of course.'

'– We've killed a lot of carrots in our time!'

'– Pulled the green leafy heads off the little beggars!'

'– Crunched them to smithereens!'

'– Forced them through a grater!'

'– Boiled them!'

'– Smoked them!'

The other Bunnies looked at Bunny Seven. 'Only once,' he said. 'By mistake.'

The King considered. 'All right, bunnies,' he said. 'Show me how you would deal with a carrot attack.'

Credulous said, 'Ah – your Majesty – we didn't bring any carrots with us. But we could show you our Ninja Parrot Routine and just pretend the parrots are carrots.'

'That's evil,' the King said. He looked at the other judges. 'Do any of you want to see parrots sliced up by a lot of chainsaws?'

The horse raised a hoof.

'We're not doing that,' said the King. 'We need real carrots. Does anyone in the audience have a carrot?'

Silence. Then the horse hesitantly raised a hoof again. And fell over again.

'All right,' said the King. 'Someone get the horse's carrots. And then put the horse in prison.'

Prince Credulous now had a barrelful of carrots. The Bunnies were juggling their chainsaws. The carrots began to fly and were shredded by the saws. Next the food processors came out; then an assortment of hammers and crowbars; lastly, the Bunnies dropped their weapons and attacked the flying carrots using Karate, Judo, Taekwondo and Yoga.

'Yoga?' asked the King.

'Yeah,' said the Head Bunny. 'We put our minds into an exalted state and imagine the carrots aren't there. And then, all of a sudden, they aren't.'

'You're just eating them!' one of the judges accused.

'Uh – it **looks** like we're eating them when we do Yoga. But we're really absorbing them into Universal Consciousness. We become the Mind of Carrot.'

It was certainly the case that all the carrots had disappeared. In their place was a bowl of salad, some yummy cakes and a pot of creamy orange-coloured soup.

The judges tried the food.

'You've got the job,' said the King. 'Little Beauty will be safe in your – paws.'

Carrot guardians

Their job was simple: keep orange pointy vegetables away from Beauty for a year, starting on her 10th birthday. If she could get through twelve months without pricking her finger on a carrot, she would be free from the witch's curse.

'But what *is* the witch's curse?' asked Prince Credulous in their first meeting with the royal family.

The Queen said, 'It's – oh golly - the witch never said, did she?'

'She never got that far,' said the King. 'She got carroted halfway through.'

'I was too young to remember,' said sweet little Beauty, tossing her cute golden curls.

'Duh!' said older sister Duty. 'Think about it: what name was Beauty christened with?'

'Sleeping Beauty,' said the Queen. 'After her Greataunt Sleeping.'

'Oh,' said Beauty. 'Wasn't that just asking for trouble?'

The Bunnies loved little Beauty. They accompanied her on all her royal visits and guarded her room at night. They played hopscotch with her, as well as other happy – and hoppy - games.

'Are you sure there's really seven of you?' asked the Princess one day.

'Yeah - we move so fast, no one can see us properly.'

She pointed at each in turn. 'One, two, three, four...

oh… I must have lost my place when counting again!'

'We love you, Princess!'

She said happily, 'Thank you. I love myself. So that makes eight of us!'

'You mean five – uh... no, you're right. Eight.'

The only person who didn't love Beauty was her big sister Duty. This wasn't surprising: Duty was given all the royal work, while Beauty got all the praise, just for being Beautiful. So when Credulous started helping Duty with her chores, she was delighted to have someone she could boss around – someone who did the cleaning and cooking and opening village fetes and launching ships, even though ships hadn't been invented yet.

After a few days, Princess Duty said to Credulous, 'I need a very tiny favour.'

'Anything!' exclaimed Credulous. 'So long as it's not wrong, of course.'

'Would I do that?' she asked sweetly. 'Just meet me at midnight behind the prison... and bring a chainsaw.'

He did as she asked, and she led him to the back of the locked and barred wooden stables there.

She said, 'My friend the horse has only a very tiny window, and it upsets him. I want you to cut a bigger opening for him.' She marked out a window that went all the way from the ground to well over head height.

'Isn't that a door you've drawn?' asked Credulous.

'Of course not. It's a very large window that will let in much more light and air. Horses *need* light and air!'

So Credulous started the chainsaw and cut along the line Duty had drawn… and the Very Large Window fell out onto the ground… and the horse stepped out of prison… and Duty leapt upon his back and rode away.

Fifteen prison guards came running and pointed their spears and swords at Credulous.

'Sorry about that,' said the ex-Prince. 'I can nail it back up if you like…'

Beauty turns 10

Beauty's birthday was on the 31st of October, and the Bunnies were in charge of guarding the doors into the Party Palace that had been built especially for her big day. They refused entry to all adults and confiscated anything orange or pointy. They now had a barrel full of oranges and some children's crayons.

Three women came to the door dressed in black and wearing tall, pointy hats with silver moons, stars and carrot shapes painted on them.

'No grown ups allowed,' said one of the Bunnies.

The three said sweetly in chorus, 'Oh, but we're just very tall children!'

'Yeah? Well, we don't like tall children with old faces and scary hats. So you're outnumbered, seven to three.'

'But there's only four of you!'

'We *definitely* don't like big kids who can't count.'

'– We like cutting kids like you down to size.'

'– Yeah! Because we like Peace and Happiness!'

'– Peace and Happiness!'

'– Equal rights for small kids!'

The Bunnies opened their violin cases and started up

their chainsaws. The three witches looked worried. One of them said:

'It's only our hats that make us seem tall.'

A Bunny suggested, 'Take your hats off, then.'

'Ooooo we couldn't do *that*, no. These are our party hats for Halloween!'

'Halloween hasn't been invented yet!'

The witches chorused, 'Then why are the children dressed as ghosts and ghouls and goblins and other scary things starting with G?'

'Because none of those things have been invented yet, either. So take off your hats, or –'

Seven chainsaws were waved in their direction.

'– Or we'll have to cut them off!'

The three witches screamed in chorus and ran away. One of their hats fell off and a lot of sharpened carrots fell out of it.

'Awwww, we scared the poor kids,' said a Bunny.

'I feel a bit mean now,' said another.

'But they couldn't count. What do they teach kids at school these days?'

'Yeah, I blame the teachers.'

While the Bunnies were protecting Beauty from a pointy hat attack, the birthday party was going on inside. There was a lovely orange vegetable cake made by Duty, topped with cute orange crunchy candles sharpened to a point.

'You're such a tease, Duty!' said Prince Credulous.

'They look just like carrots!'

'Would I do that?' she asked.

'Of course not!'

They played plenty of party games organised by Duty, such as pin the orange pointy tail on the donkey (which the donkey didn't like at all), pass the pointy orange parcel, and spin the bottle thingy that's orange and pointy. Beauty loved the games; the Bunnies loved eating the leftovers; Prince Credulous loved gazing at Duty as she organised it all.

'You're such a good sister!' he exclaimed.

'I'd be even better as an only child!' she said.

The following days went by smoothly, with no sign of a carrot attack. The Bunnies enjoyed their work and they loved the little treats that Duty made for her sister: orange-coloured crisps, frozen orange ice lollies, crunchy salad buffets with shredded spiky orange toppings, and some useful orange toothpicks.

On Saturdays, Duty spent happy mornings galloping through the countryside on her horse. Prince Credulous often went with her on his own horse, and would help her bring back large bags of crunchy orange vegetables.

He said, 'You know, these look awfully like carrots!'

Duty laughed. 'Silly Credulous! They're just parsnips with sunburn.'

The first witch

Then the curse struck. Little Beauty was wandering through the palace, following a treasure map her big sister had drawn for her. She came to a room she had never seen before, high in the attic.

In the room was a young lady all dressed in black,

wearing a pointy black hat and sitting at a spinning wheel. She had a spindle in her hand, shaped like a... well, shaped like an orange pointy vegetable that Beauty didn't know the name of. She was using it to prepare the yarn for spinning, but she wasn't doing it very well and the wool kept getting tangled.

'Ohhhhh!' said Beauty. 'You're – no, don't tell me, let me guess – you're building a space rocket!'

The lady cackled, 'No, little girl. Rockets haven't been invented yet! I'm spinning wool to make lovely sweaters with! Would you like to try doing it?'

Beauty shook her head. 'That looks *boring*. Anyway, I can buy all the sweaters I want in shops. I could buy the whole shop if I wanted: I'm a princess, you know.'

The woman shouted, 'You're a princess, hey? Well, I'm one of the three daughters of the witch who was carroted at your christening! And now I'm going to have my revenge!'

'Oh,' said Beauty. 'So you're not really an old-fashioned wool spinner? That explains why you're not very good at it.'

The witch screeched, 'You nasty little slop bucket! You pig-snout! You unkind judge of my spinning abilities! I'll show you!'

She picked up the sharpened carrot spindle.

Just then the Easter Bunnies burst in through the door, seven roaring chainsaws clutched in their paws. 'Put down that carrot, evil spinning woman!' they shouted.

The witch laughed and threw the carrot. But the Bunnies threw their chainsaws, which spun and buzzed through the air, shredding the carrot to smithereens and bouncing across the floor towards the spinning wheel, which the saws carved into a model of an Eiffel Tower that hadn't been invented yet, before landing in the witch's lap and various other places.

This is a chainsaw

There was a certain amount of screaming.

'Oooops,' said the Bunnies.

Beauty said, 'She doesn't look so nice without a head.'

The second witch

A month later, little Beauty was following another treasure map drawn by her lovely big sister. The trail led through the garden and into a cave, past a notice that read DANGER DO NOT ENTER, past a second notice that read TURN AROUND NOW and then a third that read YOU'RE DEAD.

Beauty laughed. 'It's just like Duty to make the Treasure Hunt exciting!'

At the end of the tunnel was a grotto lit by a smoking torch. Beneath the torch was a second lady dressed in black with a pointy hat on her head. She had a tall, funny-shaped barrel in front of her, with a long wooden stick poking out from the top of it. She was plunging the stick up and down, rather too hard, and there was a lot of cream spilt upon the floor.

'Ohhhhh!' said Beauty. 'You're – no, don't tell me, let me guess – you're making frozen milk shakes!'

The lady cackled, 'No, little girl. Those haven't been invented yet. I'm churning cream to turn it into butter! Would you like to try it? Look, I have a lovely orange pointy thing to scrape the butter off the sides with.'

Beauty shook her head. 'That looks *boring*. Anyway, I can buy all the butter I want in shops. I could buy a whole dairy if I wanted: I'm a princess, you know.'

The woman shouted, 'You're a princess, hey? Well, I'm another of the three daughters of the witch who was carroted at your christening! And now I'm going to have my revenge!'

'Oh,' said Beauty. 'So you're not really a dairy maid? That explains why you're rubbish at churning.'

The witch screeched, 'You nasty little fish-faced slug-sucker! You unkind judge of my churning abilities! Take *that*!'

She picked up the sharpened carrot to throw.

Just then the Easter Bunnies burst in through the door, their roaring chainsaws in their hands. 'Put down the carrot, evil churning woman!' they shouted.

The witch laughed and threw the carrot. But the Bunnies threw their chainsaws, which spun and buzzed through the air, shredding the carrot to smithereens and then bouncing across the floor towards the butter churn, which the saws carved into a model of a Statue of Liberty that hadn't been invented yet, before ….

There was a certain amount of screaming.

'Oooops.'

Beauty said, 'Oh. Right down the middle. That must have really hurt.'

It was now almost the time that would have been Christmas, if it had been invented yet. Snow was falling and presents were being wrapped. Prince Credulous was working on his own present for Princess Duty: a poem. He had got as far as…

Duty

Is such a cutie

… but then he'd got stuck, so he decided to ask Duty what she thought of it so far. He trudged through the snow to the stables and found her there, crying.

'What's wrong, dear Princess Duty?' he asked.

'Nothing!' she said fiercely.

'Oh… That's all right then.'

'Grrr!' exclaimed Duty. 'When a woman says *Nothing* is wrong, what she really means is *Something* is wrong, but she's not going to tell you!'

'Oh… That's all right then.'

'Double grrrr!' exclaimed Duty. 'When a woman says she's *Not* going to tell you, what she really means is she *Wants* to tell you, and is waiting for you to ask.'

'Oh,' said a puzzled Credulous. He asked again, 'What's wrong, dear Princess Duty?'

'My stupid sister! Everyone loves her and no one loves me - just because she's pretty and I'm not.'

'But that's not right,' said Credulous. '*I* love you! And I've written a poem about how cute you are!'

'Have you?' she asked shyly.

'Yes, and it's the longest poem I've ever written. Listen: *Duty… Is such a cutie.* Do you like it so far?'

'It's the best poem I've ever heard,' sighed Duty. 'And I'm going to forgive little Beauty for being so beautiful. She can't help it.'

'Oh good.'

'And I'll stop trying to poke her with carrots, too.'

'Oh… You weren't really doing that, were you?'

'You're so credulous, Credulous.'

'Thank you! Will you marry me?'

Princess Duty retorted, 'I can't possibly marry someone who believes everything I say!'

Credulous thought very hard about this. Then his face lit up. 'I don't believe you!' he shouted happily.

'Good answer!' laughed Duty. 'So I *will* marry you. But first we have to save Beauty from the witch.'

Third time unlucky

But it was too late. While Credulous was holding Duty's hand and reading her the poem for the fifth time, little Beauty was following yet another Treasure Map drawn by her sister. She walked out of the castle and through a dark snowy wood, then into a small clearing.

The clearing was full of snowmen, all standing stiffly with their stubby hazel branch arms sticking out at odd angles, their coal-black eyes glittering and their carrot noses pointing... all except for one snowman, which didn't have a nose.

'Poor snowman!' exclaimed Beauty softly. 'You look so sad without a pointy orange nose like your friends!'

The snowman nodded gloomily and a tiny tear ran down one cheek before freezing there.

Just then, a lady wearing a black cloak and a pointy black hat stepped out from the shadows of the trees. She asked in a sweet voice, 'Would you like to put a nose on the snowman, little girl?'

by Marta

'Yes please, Nice Lady who can't possibly be a witch because she has a kind voice.'

'Come here then, little girl who can't possibly be as gullible as she seems. I have a carr- I mean a pointy orange nose – for you to put on the sad snowman.'

Just then the Bunnies came running through the woods, starting their chainsaws and shouting, 'Step away from the snowman, evil carrot-nosing woman!'

But the witch simply laughed and snapped her fingers. The snowmen began moving. They slid slowly towards the Bunnies, their branch arms clawing, their pebble mouths chomping.

The Bunnies ran to meet them, swinging chainsaws in perfect harmony, carving the most wonderful snow sculptures of Loony Tunes cartoons that hadn't been invented yet. They worked their way through Tweety and Sylvester and Bugs Bunny and Roadrunner and Daffy Duck before the saws began to freeze up. All seven chainsaws jammed part way through Wylie Coyote, which is a shame because for the first time ever, he had almost caught the poor frozen Roadrunner.

Still the snowmen advanced. Behind them, the witch had snatched Princess Beauty and was laughing with so much glee that she dropped her carrot into the snow.

The Bunnies took out their flamethrowers and melted a path through the snow army. The witch was feeling about in the snow for her carrot – *ah, there it was!* – she was picking it up - she was about to prick Beauty's finger with it – when there was a whinnying and a galloping: and a big snowball came whizzing through the air and knocked the witch flat onto her back.

'And there's more where that came from, Witch!' shouted Princess Duty from the back of her horse, her arms loaded with snowballs Credulous had made for her. 'Don't you *dare* touch my precious little sister!'

The witch sat up. A snowball knocked off her hat. Another one knocked the carrot from her hand. She screeched and pulled a wand from her cloak. 'You can't stop me, Duty! My mother's spell can't be undone! Little Beauty *will* prick her finger on a carrot and then – well, I don't know what will happen, but it'll be nasty!'

She raised her wand. Duty threw another snowball; it

halted in midair. Prince Credulous threw one; he hit Duty by mistake. The Bunnies' flamethrowers ran out of gas. It looked like curtains for Beauty – or rather, it looked like Carrots, followed by a 100 year snoozathon.

But the Princess's horse gave a whinny. He turned around and aimed a kick at the nearest snowman. Its carrot nose flew through the air... high in the air... the carrot began to drop towards the witch.

'You can't get me that way!' screeched the witch. 'I've got my eye on that carrot! I won't be taken by surprise like my mother was! I've got my eye on it –'

There was a certain amount of screaming, and then a lot of silence.

'Oh,' said little Beauty. 'Right in the eye. Ouch.'

'Bet she didn't see that coming,' said Bunny Seven.

'Uh - she did, actually,' said the other Bunnies.

An enchanted sleep

Soon Duty was handing round sandwiches back at the palace. 'Dear little Beauty is safe at last,' she said.

'And I owe it all to you!' said little Beauty to Princess Duty. 'You're such a good sister. And you make such lovely orange pointy sandwiches!'

'Have some salad to go with them,' suggested Credulous, just as the King and Queen entered the room.

Bad timing.

'Yummy!' said Beauty, reaching into the salad bowl...

'... *Ouch!*' she cried. 'I pricked my finger on an orange pointy thing!'

'Uh oh....' They all looked at her with concern.

'I'm perfectly all right,' she said. 'I don't know why you're making such a fuss!'

'Oh no,' said her sister, Princess Duty. 'I'm feeling very tired all of a sudden...'

Then Duty fell asleep with her head in the salad bowl.

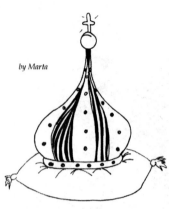

by Marta

'Oh dear,' said the King. 'Now someone has to kiss Princess Duty and wake her. That's the rule.'

'*I'll do it!*' exclaimed Credulous.

'No you won't!' retorted the Queen. 'You're the one who passed the salad bowl to little Beauty and told her to have some. We all heard you.'

'Exactly,' said the King. 'So *you're* going to prison. Someone else will have to kiss Princess Duty.'

The horse gave a hopeful whinny and held up one hoof before falling over. A lot of carrots fell out of its saddle bags.

'Ha!' said the King. '*You're* going to prison, too.'

The King and Queen looked at the Easter Bunnies.

'We're not kissing her,' said the Head Bunny.

'- We know what happens when you kiss princesses.'

'- Yeah, romance and flowers and things like that.'

'- Happily ever after stuff.'

'- Lots of holding hands and sighing.'

'- No more chainsaws or machine guns.'

'- Yuk!'

The King said, 'Then *you're* going to prison as well.'

'Hooray! That isn't half as bad as romance,' the Bunnies said with relief.

And so they were all taken off to prison. Prince Credulous had to share a cell with the horse, which is as messy as it sounds.

The Bunnies didn't mind being in prison because that meant they had more time for inventing things: such as tunnelling machines, dynamite and carrot chocolate.

A face from the past

A proclamation was sent to neighbouring kingdoms:

Wanted
A handsome prince to kiss a sleeping princess
in exchange for:
her hand in marriage
plus a lifetime supply of carrots.

Note to applicants: Princess Duty is no Beauty. She is usually difficult and always stubborn. She has a heart of gold, a fist of steel and a range of unusual hairstyles.

PS - She may not be pretty, but she IS rich.

After a month, just one prince wrote back to say he would come do the kissing: and it was someone they least expected.

Prince Usurper rode through the castle gates and was taken to the King. After the usual royal handshakes and cups of tea, he was shown around the palace gardens and was allowed to try out the slide in Princess Beauty's playground before being taken around the dungeons.

'Oh I say!' he exclaimed as they peered into one prison cell. 'Is that *you*, Credulous, old chap?'

'Usurper!' Credulous said. 'What are *you* doing here?'

'I'm here to kiss a princess, Creddy boy!' Usurper said.

Credulous said, 'But – but – but you're already married to the lovely Princess Mendacious.'

'Sadly not,' sighed Usurper. 'The day we were married, she said she wouldn't trade me for all the Zithers in Zululand; but the next day she met a rich old King who had zillions of gold coins... and *she left me*, Creddy: can you believe it?'

'Poor Usurper,' said Credulous kindly. 'I know how it feels.'

'Ah well,' said Usurper. 'It wasn't *that* bad: I had her

head chopped off. *Vengeance* is my middle name, you know! And now I'm going to marry that rich Princess Duty: I'm kissing her awake tomorrow morning!'

'No!' said Credulous. 'You can't! That's so Unfair!'

'Ha ha!' laughed Usurper. 'That's my *other* middle name. And by the way…'

He leaned close and whispered, 'You remember that nurse who said you and I had been swapped at birth? She was lying. Princess Mendacious and I *paid* her to say that. Clever plan, hey? Three witches suggested it to me. Ha ha! And the nurse won't be able to take it back, because I had *her* head chopped off too! *Double* ha ha!'

A defining kiss

Later that evening, Credulous was complaining to Beauty through the bars of his cell. 'I won't let him take another princess from me! I must escape. I *must!*'

'Really?' asked Princess Beauty. 'I thought you liked it here, and that's why you were staying. The Bunnies have been out for ages. Shall I ask them to send you some carrot chocolate? It's scrummy!'

As dawn fell upon the unsuspecting kingdom, filling it with light and birdsong and worried early worms, four Bunnies got out of their tunnelling machine and attached dynamite to some stone slabs above them.

A few minutes later, there was a small explosion. Then a horse fell on them, followed by a prince.

An hour later, they were chainsawing their way through the wall of the chamber where Princess Duty was snoring soundly.

The wall fell; they ran inside; but they were too late. Prince Usurper had just bowed low to the King and Queen and was walking towards the four poster bed at the far end of the snore-filled room.

'Stop!' shouted Credulous. 'You mustn't kiss Duty! *I'm* the man for that!'

Usurper kept walking but called back, 'Hullo there, Creddy boy! Don't worry – I was just tucking her in, you know. Don't want her to catch cold, do we?'

'Oh,' said Credulous. 'That's very kind of you.'

Usurper hurried over to the bed before turning back and sneering, 'Really, Credulous, you are so – so *credulous*! Of *course* I'm going to kiss her and wake her and marry her, and probably have her head cut off at some point. And there's *nothing* you can do about it.'

'Oh yes, there is!' shouted four voices.

Usurper said sharply, 'No, there isn't!'

The Head Bunny said, 'We've got chainsaws. We'll slice off your lips and feed them to the royal goldfish.'

Usurper said, '*Not* worried. You'll be a kiss too late!'

This is a bunny by Maverick

He bent to kiss the Princess, but Bunny Seven shouted, 'Wait! I've got it!'

'Got *what*?' shouted the angry Usurper, pausing with his lips halfway to their target.

'Got a dictionary here,' said Seven. 'And it says there's all sorts of kissin'. Such as –'

He whispered something to Credulous.

'Really?' asked Credulous. 'Would a kiss like that count? I find that hard to believe.'

'That'd be a first,' sneered Usurper as he bent again to kiss Princess Duty. But he'd waited a moment too long. As his face approached Duty's, her eyes opened suddenly and the lovely smile that had just appeared on her face turned into a scowl: and then she head-butted him on the nose.

'Ouch! That's a kind of kissin' too,' said Seven, showing the other Bunnies "*Glasgow Kiss*" in the dictionary.

Princess Duty sat up and… blew a kiss back to Credulous, in return for the one he had earlier blown to her.

Meanwhile, a dazed Usurper was staggering about the chamber, his eyes crossed, his hands over his aching nose, trying to plant a kiss on the twenty Duties he was now seeing.

First he tried to kiss the Queen.

Then he tried to kiss a guard.

Then he succeeded in kissing the King.

And the horse.

He tried to kiss little Beauty, who screamed and ran away: so he skipped across the room after her and tried to kiss the Bunnies, but tripped over a big dictionary on the floor and fell onto a buzzing chainsaw and then…

'Oh dear,' said Princess Beauty. 'I don't think my sister will want to marry the bits that are left…'

'Definitely not!' said Princess Duty. 'He's not half the man he used to be!'

Hoppy endings

Princess Duty married Prince Credulous and they rode off into the sunset together.

Watching them go, Princess Beauty sighed. 'That's so romantic,' she said to the Bunnies.

'No it isn't!' the Bunnies insisted hurriedly.

'And *you're* all so romantic!' the Princess added.

'No we aren't!' said the shocked Bunnies.

'Wait.... Maybe we are,' said Bunny Seven, taking out his dictionary. 'Oh yeah. Romantic also means Fanciful and Imaginative and Adventurous. That's us!'

'Excellent!' sighed Beauty. 'So one of you *has* to marry me. The end.'

And if you want to know more about the Bunnies – and their involvement with Snow White, Cinderella and Bad Santa – you'll have to read Wicked Tales One, Two and Three.

Some other books by Ed Wicke for ages 8 and over...

WICKED TALES Nine crazy stories. Did you know that the bears think *Goldilocks* is a stupid story and have their own version? Or that lightning is made by a family of trolls living in the clouds? What happens when Alicroc the Alien becomes a teacher at a nursery school? How does a dancing horse save a fairy from a witch? Why does Snow White team up with the 7 Easter Bunnies, and why do they have machine guns?

WICKED TALES TWO Chock full of crazy characters. Gangster rats and a cute baby... Jack, the Giant, the Ogress, the cow, the magic chicken and the magic hat... Alicroc the Alien scoutmaster... The Bad Tooth Fairy, the Tooth Mice and the Toenail Fairy... The Gorilla tricks the Hunter, with help from a Singing Snake... Cinderella, the Fairy Grotmother and the 6 Easter Bunnies clean up at the Palace!

WICKED TALES THREE Robbie has been trapped by a witch inside a book of short stories. In order to escape, he changes all her scary stories into funny, crazy ones... Red Riding Hood, Grandma and the Wolf take on the evil Piggy Bankers... Bad Santa has a plan to steal Santa's special teddies... with the help of five well-armed Easter Bunnies... Billy the Bully goes fishing - but he's the one who gets caught, by Gutsy the Shark. ... A sweet baby and a good puppy meet the evillest kitten in the world ... Gina and Harry meet a sweet-looking grandmotherly lady who lives in a cottage made of very old gingerbread ... Baby Human's parents are thrilled when Sir William Wolf invites them all to his party ... The three Trolls are very hungry, and very, very stupid. Will they eat the Princess before Davy can save her?

THE GAME OF PIRATE When fifteen year old orphan Jack Hampton pays a final visit to Captain Jones in prison, he doesn't expect to spend the next few months aboard the Firebird with a crew of rugged pirates, the fearsome, mysterious Madame Helena and a manuscript full of puzzling clues. An exciting tale of pirates, treasure, treachery and adventure: all somehow tangled up with the loss of the Curchan Ruby and an unusual board game, the Game of Pirate.

BILLY JONES, KING OF THE GOBLINS Billy Jones has the same sort of problems you have - a grandma who's loopy, a school bully who wants to thump him, and a mean teacher who insists he'll have to do the school's country dancing display dressed as a girl! But on his tenth birthday he's woken at midnight by a group of weird goblins who tell him he's now their king. You *know* it's going to get crazier by the minute...

AKAYZIA ADAMS AND THE MASTERDRAGON'S SECRET A school visit to London Zoo causes Kazy Adams to swap the rough streets of London for a new world of magic, adventure and danger. And in Old Winsome's Academy, there's an ancient mystery to solve: the disappearance of nine pupils during the Headship of the Masterdragon Tharg, at the time of the Goblin Wars.

AKAYZIA ADAMS AND THE MIRRORS OF DARKNESS The second adventure of Akayzia Adams and her friends starts with one mirror and ends with another. In between, there are three worlds of magic, a squadron of werewitches, a fistful of trolls, and one annoying little lizard with a taste for chocolate. And in the Academy, there are thousands of spiders... some of them not spiders at all.

MATTIE AND THE HIGHWAYMEN It's 1845. Recently orphaned and running away from her bullying aunt, 13-year-old Matilda Harris finds herself down in The Devil's Eyeball with an eccentric, well-spoken highwayman; his gang Lump, Stump, Pirate and Scarecrow; and two young "brats" who have escaped from the notorious Andover Workhouse.

BULLIES The only book in the world with a fairy who conducts anti-bully warfare using beetles, a snowman who talks in riddles, a school assembly taken by a talking bear, a little sister who starts a pirate mutiny at school and a boy who turns into a bird after Christmas lunch! A book packed with poems and riddled with riddles. A book that's serious about bullying... but *crazy* about everything else!

NICKLUS There's a mad scientist who wants to destroy all the cats in England, and nobody can stop her – except Nicklus and Marlowe. Nicklus is a nine year old boy who hardly talks at all. Marlowe is a talking cat, the "coolest cat in England". Together they set out on an adventure to find Nicklus' missing mother and save the cats.